THE MAKING OF
A STANDUP COMEDIAN

. . . a tale of a prankster who hones his comedy writing skills at his work place, the home improvement store, by telling his jokes to anybody who will listen and the 'dream he had' to compete in the 'America's got Talent' competition that could catapult him to fame, fortune, and groupies of women. You will laugh till the tears run down your legs!!

By the way, here's a copy of Jimmy's resume taken from his social media web sites, no job too small or too big he won't tackle:

Occupation: Author, Graveyard Digger, Gun For Hire, Bank Robber, Hit Man, Con Man, Secret Agent Man, Cowboy, Dancer For Money, Mooner For Hire, News Reporter, Junk Collector, Wheeler/Dealer, Organ Stealer, Pole Dancer, Ass Kisser, Scam Artist, Junk Food Junkie, Kidnapper of Pets, Chef, Great Pretender, Handy Man, Streaker, Insurance Con Man, Prospector For Oil, Inventor, Your Man, A Bag of Chips (twinkies, ho ho, scooter pie, ding dong, gummy bears all rolled into one), America's got Talent Wannabe Winner, and whatever else you want me to be!

Ps:
I can be had, just show me the money and call me Suga. No, I'm Jimmy, you're Suga!!!

THE MAKING OF
A STANDUP COMEDIAN

JIMMY CORREA

iUniverse LLC
Bloomington

The Making of A Standup Comedian

iUniverse books may be ordered through booksellers or by contacting:

iUniverse LLC
1663 Liberty Drive
Bloomington, IN 47403
www.iuniverse.com
1-800-Authors (1-800-288-4677)

ISBN: 978-1-4917-1090-6 (sc)
ISBN: 978-1-4917-1089-0 (e)

Printed in the United States of America.

iUniverse rev. date: 10/18/2013

Dedicated to all my friends, family members, and those 13 women of mine; but if you take into consideration that wives 5, 9, and 11 are the same lady, then it's eleven.

☞ MY ACKNOWLEDGMENT

There are so many people I would like to thank. Let me start off by saying I could not have done it without the social media web sites that include: You Tube, Face Book, and Pinterest. Through my sharing of songs, videos, prank stories, photos, and writings I am achieving my dreams of stardom. I must also give a shout out to my friends from across the pond, Maggie and Marisol, who through their initial responses to my stories in 'You Tube' brought me a ton of laughs and encouragement. I can't thank them enough, and god bless all my faithful supporters, including some who thought it couldn't be done. Love you all,

Jimmy!!!

PLEASE NOTE:

This is a fictional account of a dream I had to participate in the 'America's got Talent' TV Show competing against the best that America's got to offer in hopes of winning the grand prize. Many of the events mentioned are not true, nor did any of the celebrity judges, hosts, or producers make or take part in the actions mentioned within.

Heck, I'm still undecided if I'm ever going to compete in the show. I've never told a joke in front of more than eight folks at one time, never mind a couple thousand in a live audience or on national TV in front of millions of people worldwide. Like Ralph Kramden, I would hummmmmmmmer hummmmmmmmer till I pee all over myself due to stage fright . . .

I hope I brighten up your day and make you laugh, that is all I intended to do when I put this book together. Also I'm more of a story teller like my idols before me, Abraham Lincoln, Mark Twain, Will Rogers, Richard Pryor, Flip Wilson, George Carlin, and Robin Williams. Thanks and god bless us all,

Jimmy, the Story Teller!!!

☛ INTRODUCTION

Yes, Jimmy Correa is at it again! His previous literary works 'How My Prank Stories In 'You Tube' Made Me An Overnight Sensation, Well Almost' and 'How My Prank Stories In Social Media Web Sites Got Me Committed In The Psychiatric Ward At Bellevue Hospital' was not enough. This time he takes it up a notch and tries his hand as a standup comedian. And hopes and prays he doesn't have to beat some heckler to death if she dares to interrupt him as he works his craft. Here let Jimmy speak for himself:

For many years friends of mine have always thought I was either crazy or funny. I would like to think crazy funny is more like it. And here I am attempting to do standup comedy. I must be crazy after all because I would die in a heartbeat. Who do you know in their right mind wants to hear 'a nobody' lecture them about the facts of life? Yes, this is a compilation of my life. I tell about my golden years, my youth, my school days, and the time spent on the streets of NYC, diddy bopping with the wild boys, or playing stick ball, skelzies, and best of all, hop scotch with the girls.

I talk about my romantic sides, later of my work places including when I worked at Merrill Lynch that one time Wall Street prestigious firm buying and selling everything including stocks and bonds, treasuries, money markets, annuities, commodities, and eventually that toxic junk. Also, I tell of my tenure at the ING Service Center in Minot, ND making face increases, face decreases, beneficiary changes, address changes, adding child riders, and collateral assignments etc. on insurance policies. But that's not all; during my breaks you would find me chasing beaver (the two legged kind, don't ask) and rabbits or deer for dinner because one of my ex-wives had a craving for free meat. Now in my current tour of duty as we speak I work at a local Home Depot Store here in NYC where they got me selling nipples and ball cocks in the plumbing aisles. My mother would disown me or beat me silly if she knew. But then that's where I had my opportunity to be on stage, and hone my skills as a story teller. Sometimes the customers would walk away scratching their heads saying, "He should be on TV or behind locked bars, because that boy aint wrapped too tight, who the heck let him out of the psychiatric ward?"

Don't laugh, many of them come back looking for me to tell them some more? So who's the crazy one? And that's when I knew I was in the wrong business, I should be on stage perfecting my craft as a comedian and charging people a fee for my services. I could tell them of my arm transplant therefore the reason I was wearing long sleeve shirts in the dead of summer because I didn't want anybody to notice I had received my deceased wife's arm. Why it was five inches shorter, smoother than a baby's butt, hairless like just out of a Brazilian waxing parlor, and prettier than the other arm. Maybe I should have gotten both arms, darn it, I blew it but who knew.

Or the time a NYC Fire Department ambulance driver nearly pushed me off the road because he had a whole bunch of toes to deliver. Oh, you don't want to know! Let's not forget that dispute I had with a lady bus driver because she called me a moron. Oooooooh I wanted to beat her silly with my slippers! Well it's all here and much more. So if you got nothing better to do sit back, get comfortable, get you a drink, make mine tequila with the worm in it ooooooooooo ooooooooooo ooooooooooo. And by all means don't choke on that beef jerky we push at the store. You might even pee on yourself laughing so hard. But then that's the price you have to pay if you want some of this. Like I always say, "no tickie, no shirtie." Well not me per say, my Chinaman at the laundry place where I hang trying to pick up lonely desperate women. Ok, ok where I hang.

Well, it's time to go, I'm rehearsing especially if I plan to make that prestigious list of who's who in show business. By the way, my manager is trying to book me a guest appearance on the Oprah Winfrey Show. Who knows, maybe Oprah will take me home to her fancy crib, and rock me away ooooooooooooooooo weeeeeeeeeeeeeee. Did I mention I'm a hunk waiting to happen? Well, let Oprah tell you all about me in her memoirs chapter 'Big Jim.' Wait till she meets the kid, oh, that's moi. What's moi, me, in French or Swahili, ciao Jimmy, aka Mr. Standup!!!

(Opening scene at Jimmy's workplace, the home improvement store located on 73-01 somewhere in the heart of the big apple in NYC, where you'll find him in plumbing aisles six, seven, and thirty doing shelf maintenance, inventory control, cleaning, assisting customers with their questions, purchases, and last but not least, telling them prank stories)

Jimmy's a pro at this, no not plumbing, heck he can't even screw a screw and the idea of getting his hands dirty that would kill him. He loves telling prank stories and always looks for the right moment to sneak in a joke or two. He spots a lady customer and proceeds to acknowledge her The Home Depot way. "Hello, how may I help you, what project are you working on?" When he's finally through he asks her if it's okay to ask a lady he just met if he can paint her toe nails, and then she paints his toe nails, and then they paint up the town red. She smiles and says "sure why not," and they both burst out laughing. Another time Jimmy notices a fella strolling down his aisle with his hands in his pockets and tells him that old Confucius proverb "Man on street corner with hands in pockets, he's not crazy, just feeling little nuts." That immediately prompts the man to pull his hands out of his pockets, smile and chuckle while walking away thinking Jimmy should be locked up in a mental institution. Oh, this goes on all day long, sometimes he'll say it in front of two or three customers and if they come back he'll tell them another and then another. One time he pulled in a crowd of eight customers. He made their day. After Jimmy was finished, he wanted so much to take off his hat and pass it around. But then that would be grounds for job termination, if caught. Those Atlanta folks watching the thirty or more cameras throughout the store would have a field day, fuhgettaboudit!!!

Now Jimmy has to be careful when telling his stories that he's not observed by the store manager, the assistant store managers, or the department heads. But if he is spotted then that's when he'll pull an item from a nearby shelf and pretend he's giving customers pointers on the use and installation of that item. "Yes folks this is a nipple, no not what you're thinking." "Get your mind out of the gutter." "You can stick it in a pipe and make that pipe longer like a gas pipe, water line or some shit or use it to simply connect two pipes together." Or he'll grab a plunger. "Yes folks you crouch down a bit in front of that clogged up toilet and you pump this here stick silly till you can't no more and 99.99% of the time that will do the trick unless you got a load that's over your head." He is so cool and a salesman if ever. He'll sell you the Brooklyn Bridge if he could but then that's for a later story. You'll die laughing. Just wait till you read all about it unless you were the one he scammed, hey, shit happens.

Today Jimmy's only working half a shift, "that's all she wrote" so he says. The store hires many employees and it's the part-timers that get their hours cut but then he's used to this. That's another reason why he has to make it big so one day he can finally tell the boss to shove it where it don't shine. He made that mistake once before and then had to kiss her ass to get it back. Don't remind him. You'll read all about it later. In the meantime this job helps pay the bills and his acting lessons. Jimmy can't wait till he makes it big. Minimum wage aint cutting it. He wants a piece of that pie in the sky.

Well, it's time to go. It's been a long grueling nonstop day. Jimmy's smiling from ear to ear as he runs to punch out at the time clock, and then makes a mad rush to catch the

Q47 bus that will depart within the next five minutes or so. He's got it timed just right as always. Don't be fooled he's got a method for his madness. You never know what he's got up his sleeve besides his late beloved wife's arm. Again, that's another story; wait until you read all about it.

Before we go any further let me tell you something briefly about Jimmy. He was born on a military base at the Panama Canal Zone, and would become an Army Brat for the first eight years of his life. The youngest of four children, and the only son was raised in a strict disciplinary household. No doubt it was his father's doings. He's lived most of his entire life in NYC. When he graduated from high school he would turn down two lucrative college scholarships to go into the workforce so he could mingle with his friends, put some spending loot into his pitiful empty pockets, and party hearty. A few years later, he would marry and divorce. I don't know how many times? He won't say, because he's changed his name I don't know how many times to elude those women. He's now an author, and at the present a wannabe standup comedian. He lives with his daughter who is his manager. She is a whole lot funnier and crazier than him. They own a cat or should I say the cat owns them. Her name is Pookie Gyrl.

That's her photo below helping to promote one of his books and according to Jimmy she's smarter than most fifth graders and loves reading all his books!!

After work, the minute Jimmy arrives to his residence he puts on some music and hops into the shower while singing along to his favorite songs. Music is his joy and helps him to unwind from the rat race this world has turned into. He can't wait till his acting lessons pay off and then he can perform at all the venues: casinos, night clubs, hen parties, street corners, or even at a local park or bar. For the ha ha's he works his skills at Raymundo's Barber Shop & Grill on Grand Ave. and 69th Place entertaining the customers so he can get a free haircut and a hamburger in return. They always post a sign when they know he's coming in to boost up the clientele. They gather bright and early to get a seat for the free show. He brings a hat along so his manager can pass it around, after he performs, to collect donations. He calls them that so he won't have to report them as ordinary income and it's always standing room only. Just make sure you support his efforts and he doesn't mind if you take a few dollars yourself, for he knows one good turn deserves another. But he does have a ton of homeless cats he needs to feed at his doorstep not to mention Pookie Gyrl.

Once out of the shower, Jimmy is not only singing but dancing, aware that his window is wide open and assessable to outsiders longing to peep in as he puts on a show. Those horney women can't get enough of him and he doesn't mind the attention. Heck, sometimes just for laughs he goes right up to the window and moons them. Now that's something to talk about. He likes to do his James Brown impersonation with a two-step bossa-nova and a jump back three step merengue, boy is he hot today. 'Dancing with the Stars' aint got nothing over on him. He can teach them a thing or two or three, especially that Brooke girl, ooooooooooooo weeeeeeeeeeeeee!!!

The phone rings and it's his so called sweet heart, Carmela Ortiz who he met at a Bruce Springsteen concert in Jersey a few years back. She tells him that her fortune teller has told her she has to reinvent herself; therefore she has decided to end their relationship. "Your books are not selling, your comedy is going nowhere quick, and I need a man to take care of me and pamper me to death" (her exact words). She's on her way to Europe for a well-deserved vacation and to party till she drops. She's not saying but will be going with a guy she just met at the 'House of Pancakes.' He flips pancakes for a living, and is a spitting image of Enrique Iglesias Jr. with glasses. Jimmy is speechless. He thought they were the ideal couple but guess he was wrong. She bids him good bye, so long, wishes him good luck and hangs up.

Jimmy is quite devastated and speechless. That's a first because he's got a gift for gab, and you don't want to get into a confrontation with him. He will eat you up alive and spit you out. He calls his friend Eladio at the job sight to tell him the bad news.

Eladio works in the hardware department selling chains, screws, and tie downs and is obviously a lady's man with that kind of inventory, don't even ask. That's when Eladio suggests he should hire a demolition crew to knock down her house for doing him wrong. Jimmy has a smile on his face from ear to ear. Yes, yes you're right, knock it down to the ground and Eladio says "I was only kidding." No, no it's the right thing to do, I've given that woman the best year of my life and this is how she rewards me by dumping me. Well that's what I'm going to do with the exception that I'll leave the three steps leading up to her front door intact so she can still get her mail. What kind of a heartless animal do you think I am? I may be cold but heartless, no way. Jimmy hangs up and calls his most trusted companion, his friend since childhood, Mickey Jarvis, who knows a friend who knows another friend that owns a demolition service, what are friends for?

They negotiate a service fee to flatten her house down while she's away on her vacation. This will occur just before he and his daughter depart for New Orleans, sin city, for the opportunity of a lifetime to enter that 'America's got Talent' competition show, and win the grand prize. Who knows he might even meet his idol Mariah Carey Cannon and maybe sing a duet? Yep, another notch on his lipstick case, I mean belt buckle.

Chucky two fingers Cutugno is the demolition expert. Why he's called that is beyond me? He was only missing two fingers so why not call him 'three fingers' or 'eight fingers Cutugno.' He arrived early, 5 AM, and started to bang the heck out of that one floor building with the finished basement in no time with his wrecking ball he calls 'Godzilla.' You talk about finish, it took him less than twelve minutes for the four walls to come crumbling down leaving the front three steps and door entrance standing as ordered. Jimmy paid him the negotiated fee of three thousand dollars and was so overwhelmed of how good of a job 'two fingers' did. At this stage the only thing it will be good for will be as a parking lot or a pickle factory at the most, kosher would be ideal. Jimmy loves kosher, umm, umm, umm. He can only imagine the look on Carmela's face the moment she sees it on the ground. It would be like all his Christmases coming in all at once. Winner, winner chicken dinner, hahaha!!!

By the time they got to New Orleans it was estimated there would be close to three thousand entries in all the fields known to man including but not limited to: magic, dare devil stunts, acrobats, singers, dancers, ventriloquists, dog acts, and last but not least, comedy. Jimmy and his manager arrived two days ahead of schedule. So they set up a tent behind five hundred other contestants waiting to get a shot at winning the one million dollar grand prize. He gets settled in and goes through all his comedy sketch routines trying to decide which one would do the trick to win him a spot on the talent show that will send him off to Hollywood. He narrowed it down to a few including his haircutting fiasco when he and Mickey gave Mikey Lugo a haircut of a lifetime. Here, let Jimmy tell you about them:

Folks, I got a confession to reveal and it's really the start of my mischievous ways, you don't want to know. When I was eleven my friend who will remain anonymous for fear of a lawsuit, like hell he will. His name is Michael J. Jarvis who lived in building 4-03 in the projects right next to my building at 4-21 in Queens. What the 'J' stands for god only knows. Maybe jackass because he was loose like a goose and meaner than a junkyard dog. So anyway Mickey and I were going to the movies. What movie is immaterial at this point because what I am about to say is so funny yet so unbelievable. I still don't know what motivated us to do it. As we were preparing to buy a few minor things to take along: candy, soda, ice cream, popcorn, a bag of chips, Twinkies, ho ho's, two pickles, a pack of Bazooka bubble gum, we bumped into our friend Mikey Lugo. Mikey was part Greek and part Puerto Rican and not wrapped too tight, you know lights on but nobody home. He wanted to know what we were up to with all the party goods so early in the morning. So we told him of our movie plans and asked him if he cared to come along. He responded that he was on his way to the barber shop to get a haircut, and didn't have any dough; you know cabbage, other than the haircut money. That's when Mickey chimed in and said that he was in luck because Jimmy, that's me, was a professional barber. I saw what Mickey was up to so I played along. "Yeah, but I'm still in training." So Mikey, looking down at the goodies wanted so bad to go with us looked a bit hesitant but I guess going to the movies outweighed the risks so he said "Ok." So we took Mikey to Mickey's house. Mickey got his father's electric hair clippers, tied a towel around Mikey's neck, put a bowl on his noggin and sat him in the middle of the room facing a mirror. That's when we performed our very first professional haircut. Mickey started chopping away, first from the back section of Mikey's neck, then around to the right side up to and including the right sideburn. It was a bit lopsided so I took the razor, leveled it up a bit and then worked my way to the left side. Then we noticed the sideburns were uneven. One was shorter than the other, so Mickey grabbed the clippers from my hands and tried to even them out. But then the sideburns were nowhere to be found. As Mikey was looking into the mirror, he seemed as though he wanted to cry. After twenty seconds of silence, Mickey looked at me. I looked at him. We had to bite our tongues to hold back the tears of laughter. And that's when Mikey got up and said "I gotta get out of this place," not even thanking us or giving us a tip. Heck, we were doing it for free, zilch, nada but the tip part, well that was optional but kind of expected. Mikey was our best friend up until this fiasco occurred. Why a fiasco? Because we 'eff'd him up. Mikey's last words to us was—"I'm going to tell my father on you!" Well for the next two months we avoided Mikey's building in fear we might bump into his father, Mr. Lugo. We heard of his reputation as a prize fighter, and how like Rocky Balboa he beats the meat at the back of Paulie's Butcher Shop. So we walked to school the long way around, and besides we thought we could use the added six blocks exercise. To this day I tell my new acquaintances this story and it always has them rolling off of their feet. And when there's a get together, a wedding, a wake, a divorce celebration, or a bachelor party, whatever, Mickey and I always tell the story of the movie we missed all on account of Mikey. If my recollection serves me right I think it was *Tarzan, King of the Monkeys* or *The Ape Women*.

The New Orleans audience gave Jimmy a standing ovation and they couldn't stop laughing. Howie Mandel, the one and only judge to comment said "you knocked the cover off the ball." "It's a yes for me and I can speak for the others you are going to Hollywood." Mel B and Heidi Klum blew kisses at Jimmy. Howard Stern gave him the two thumbs up nod. Nick Cannon, smiling, grabs Jimmy's hand and says "I don't need a haircut but if I know anyone who does I will send them your way." And they both laugh once more.

The next morning Jimmy and his daughter head off to Hollywood for the next round of competitions that will lead the potential winners on to Radio City Music Hall in NYC for the quarter finals. Packed and raring to go, they headed out bright and early. Their game plan was to make two stopovers at some saloons and hooter bars along the way. This would keep Jimmy fine-tuned in front of mass crowds, hecklers, and last but not least, to work for food and earn a few dollars. All of the funds received would cover travel expenses.

After seven days they finally arrived to Hollywood from New Orleans but not before making those two stops as planned to entertain folks. At his first layover, Joey D's Clam House & Bar, he tells the packed crowd a bunch of stories including the one below when he was asked to join 'The Brotherhood of Men,' the Fire Fighters of New York City. Let Jimmy tell it in his own words:

Thank you, thank you, yes folks I got a story you're just not going to believe. My Irish friend Mickey J. introduced me to some of the boys down at the firehouse, Squad 288 in Maspeth, Queens last year. They all took a liking to me after telling them a few jokes, especially Captain Longhorn. He asked me if I would like to join their

'Fraternity Band of Brothers' because they could see I was all that and a bag of chips. And get this; they even wanted me to be their mascot at the St. Paddy's Day Parade here in NY in front of millions of people and on National TV. Their first ever, mascot that is. Maybe you saw me. But they also wanted me to do three things which I found quite strange. Be the last man in the parade, wear a kilt when we march down on 5th Avenue, and last but not least, moon the folks as we marched down those forty or so blocks. Now I don't know why I couldn't march alongside of them up in the front of the line. No, they say it's an honor to be the closer. They always pick an Irish celebrity to lead the parade as the 'Grand Marshall' and that I should be at the end, this way we would have both ends covered. But I don't see the lead guy mooning anybody the way they wanted me to. They said my job was the most important and unique part of the parade. He's known as 'The Closer' and not just anybody can be the closer, somebody with guts, fortitude, and cojones, whatever that means. So to be part of this awesome group of guys I decided to do it, why not; these are America's finest, the brave men and women of the NYC Fire Department. How did it go? I thought you'd never ask! I was the laughing stock of the parade and to make matters worse I was later arrested for indecent exposure. When I went to jail none of the guys showed up in my defense. Nor did they chip in to post my bail. When we went to court the judge wanted to know why I had done what I had done. I explained how I was chosen to be their first mascot ever, and become one of their 'band of brothers.' The judge said I was lied to, and that he would suspend the charges for time already served (fourteen days), and for being a nincompoop. The nerve of him calling me that. He should have said I was a hero in the line of duty. Who else would have done what I had done? Now whenever I go to the fire house they all gather around me smiling from ear to ear, laughing hysterically, patting me on the back, and saying I'm the man! So I say to them, then if I'm the man, can I do sleepovers and polish up their bells and fire trucks? They all agreed I could. How many days have I stayed over in the firehouse? Not a freaking day. They always seem to have an excuse of some kind. Like the Fire Commissioner is in town, they're having an inspection, or they're going to paint up the fire house red. Something tells me they don't want me over. Well I'm still proud to say I'm a part of them no matter what. End of story! Thank you, thank you!

The crowd goes wild and gives Jimmy a standing ovation. He'll be kicking butt in Hollywood in no time!!!
(Play Ben E. King song "Don't Play That Song")

That's Squad 288 in Maspeth Queens. The second home to the great men and women that protect our part of the city. The city that never sleeps. Queens, New York . . .

After a few more jokes he does his encore with another funny story. Here check it out:

Last week I was passing by my local pet shop store, and the sign in the window read **TALKING DOG FOR SALE.** Well, light bulbs lit up inside my head, I could make a fortune. So I go inside and there at the counter was old man Grady. So nonchalantly, I said "So what's up my man!" and he asked me—what the heck I wanted. Nothing in particular. I just hit jackpot in bingo, don't remind me, and I was thinking of buying me a dog. Got anything special? So he jumped up and said—"well I got one just right for you," meaning me. So where is it? It's in the back. So I casually strolled to the back and sure as I'm standing here telling you this story there was this mangy looking dog sitting at the corner surrounded by all those talking birds. I could have sworn I heard them chatting before I got there. So I walked over to it, and said tell me something about yourself. Then it proceeded to tell me its name was Bella. That it had worked for the CIA, the FBI, Interpol, infiltrated the Mafia, did a stint for Scotland Yard, Sherlock Holmes, not to mention the Pink Panther himself, Inspector Clouseau. All in all the dog was a spy incognito, you know, secret agent woman. I rushed to the front of the store, and asked old man Grady why you selling the dog, he replied—"it lies a lot!"

Jimmy shows them a photo of the dog. The crowd goes wild. Jimmy is in tears because he knows the audience is in the palms of his hands. They start throwing money on to the stage that even Jimmy had to bend over to help his daughter pick them all up. Something he never does because of his days at the big house. Rule # one, you never bend over when you're in jail, don't ask!!!

That's my local pet shop store with the sign that caught my eye!!!

Yep, that's Bella the talking dog! She's smarter than a whip, likes to tell my stories to anyone who will listen, even those talking birds she mingles with. She's a ham, loves all the attention and applause!!!

In their next stopover, Kansas City, they came across another popular watering hole, 'The Goose Is Wild.' It's your average hang out. It's always packed and there are plenty of acts to entertain the folks that include comedians and semi-topless dancers that draw in rowdy cowboys, motorcyclists, both males and females. Jimmy tells it better, so let him continue:

The owner of the establishment is a lady by the name of Georgette Psaila who inherited the business from her dad five years earlier. She was once the main attraction there. But decided to run the business instead. Talk about a brick house, she's a winning hand! Now she has a dozen showgirls working for her, and imports comedy acts from around the regional area. They say The Blues Brothers once performed there, also big George Wallace, Robin Williams, Whoopi Goldberg, and a handful of others. We negotiated terms, room and board, one hundred dollars per show, and all the tip monies the folks throw your way. But if you stink, don't be surprised if you get showered with tomatoes, beer cans, and tarred and feathered. I am required to do three shows a day. So we sign up for one day. We freshen up, rest, eat, and later go for a tour of the joint. Jimmy checks out the dancing girls. There's Marisol, the import from Spain who is the star attraction of the show. She's another brick house and hot to trot. Then there's Miss Gloria Gaynor no relationship to the singer Gloria Gaynor back in the disco era. Finally there's Ivanka, an import from Sweden. Nothing phony about her, blond, smart as a whip, and knows how to shake it up. The others are your average local wannabe girls. The work staff includes barmaids, bartenders, busboys, and bouncers. All handpicked and good looking. They help to bring in the clientele as well. Claudia, the hat check girl, catches my eye. She is sweet and innocent but knows how to handle the con artists that are drawn to her. I tell her some words of advice, "My daddy once said, never bring knives to a gun fight." She smiles and then I ask her if I could buy her a drink. She says maybe later. So after the tour, I go back to get ready for the first act. I showered and had a light snack. Then had ten minutes left before going on. My beloved sidekick, my daughter, is waiting on me and we go down together for that first tour of duty. The MC kindly introduces me as 'The Boy from New York City' and I'm on:

Thank you ladies and gentlemen! It's an honor to be here. As you all know in America we have a tradition that on every October 31st we get to act silly for the day. It's called Halloween. Well I have a story that will shock you. Last year I got dressed up as a 'Streaker' or should I say dressed down. So here I am with not a stitch of clothing on, on my way to a party in 'The Village' when before you could say "how's it hanging," a crowd gathers around me. They were all so impressed with the kid (that's me). They decided to join me. After about an hour or so we were all arrested for indecent exposure.

The NYPD stopped us, frisked us, what for? There was nothing to check, we were all buck naked. They threw us in paddy wagons and hauled our asses to night court. When it was my turn to speak up in my defense, and as the 'so-called ringleader.' I told the judge I was on my way to "The Freaker's Ball" when a crowd of about a hundred joined me as we roamed the streets hooting and hollering all dressed up in our birthday suits. I reminded her "this is America baby, the land of the free and I can do whatever I want to do." I removed my robe and you should have seen the expression on her face. She was aroused and then said in stuttering words "not, not in my, my court." I was sentenced to do one hundred hours of community service and fined twenty-five dollars. Later she came down to the lockup pen to wish me luck. Sure she did, just wanted to see me/it again. I knew what she was up to. So I dropped my robe so she could get another look, that horny toad. We swapped phone #'s and addresses. She said she could give me some legal pointers, hahaha! Sure, then I'll have to tip her, don't ask. I'm going to take this to the Supreme Court. What say you, is this a tradition in your neck of the woods, Halloween.

The audience applauds and many are smiling and laughing so I tell them another story:

Hey, here's one more for the road: Folks, I got something to tell you that I'm not too proud of. In my resume I tell people I was a 'Graveyard Digger.' Well that's half the story; I'm also an 'Organ Stealer.' Yep, I bury the folks in the AM. Then I go back in the PM and excavate their body parts. Why you ask? Because I can make a fortune, and like automobiles, body parts are more expensive. If you're in need of an arm, an eye, a leg, a liver, a knee that's where I come in. I pop those babies off them dead bodies, and they're yours. Can you use a new brain or a new heart because the old one is not too swift? Then I'm the one you need. I accept only cash on delivery. No IOU's. Call me if you need a body part. Referrals are accepted. So let's do business. Btw, I'm not just a thief, I'm also an organ receiver, that's right! I got an arm transplant but that's for another story, for another day. Maybe I'll tell you later but there'll be no arm twisting, hahaha, hope to see you later!

The audience goes wild, hooting, hollering, and throwing money all over the stage. At last count we took in two hundred and forty-two dollars. Not bad for thirty-five minutes of work. We go back to our room. That pretty young thing, Claudia, knocks on my door. She is smiling and says I put on an awesome show. And yes I would like to have a drink. I let her in and tell her to call the service desk, order some food and a bottle of whatever floats her boat. I excuse myself and shower. When I come back, the table is all set. I put on some soft romantic music from my iPod, I get all dressed up and before you can whistle Dixie, they come off again. Can't say no more because what two consenting adults do on their time off is nobody's business but their own, See you!!!

Three hours pass and my manager returns with her hands full. She has spent her share of the money we took in for the last two days. I introduce her to Claudia. Claudia bids us farewell because her shift starts in half an hour. She must go and prepare. We kiss and say goodbye, not before exchanging addresses and phone numbers. I too must get ready. My act goes on in one hour. I must go through my material and decide on three jokes. Check them out below:

Folks, today I want to tell you a story about blind dating. You see many individuals try to hook up with their soul-mates in numerous ways. The two most popular are through internet match sites or in bars. You know those so-called clubs where you fill out a questionnaire so the system will try to find you an ideal mate. So if you prefer tall dark and handsome, black where you never go back, hung like a brick house, those sorts of questions. Me, I would say, rich, stacked, and witty. Color, that don't matter as long as she doesn't have what I have. See when you do use those match sites you really should be honest. If you're looking for a sexy companion spit it out, or if horny is your game that too, don't beat around the bush, hahaha. Pardon the pun. I really prefer the old fashioned techniques. I hang by the tomato counters at the supermarkets. When I see a girl who I may like I might ask her if she could kindly help me choose the right tomatoes or melons because my blind grandmother sent me to get some and get some I want, hahaha. Or I do my John Wayne impersonation and try pick up a missy type gal. So as I see one coming my way I say "Ok partner, me and Corky are free and single. How's about we ride you home so these perverts don't hit up on you." How's it going? Well I never tried it. Other ways of meeting the opposite sex or the same sex is at shopping malls, at bingo halls, in the parks, at the beaches, and the most popular of all, in the bars. See that one you have to be extra careful because once you start a drinking you let your guard down, and you just might pick any ole plain Jane. By this point you're so drunk and horny anything on two legs will do. Let me tell you about my blind date. My grandmother Ida set us up. Her name was Wanda, the milkman delivery lady. I was to meet her on Saturday night. I got all dressed up, took a shower, and shaved, put on my granddaddy's Old Spice aftershave, and some new underwear. Well at least clean ones. You never know where this will take you. So I put on my jockeys or fruit of the looms skin tight briefs. That's important because then you'll impress her with that bulging lump exposed. Especially if you should hit a home run. So we meet up at a little Italian restaurant two miles away. Don't want the local folks to know we're on a date. So I ordered one slice of pizza for two and two glasses of water. Then I rapped my heart out. Told her how beautiful her eyes were and that she smelled like a rose. I threw a quarter into the jukebox and put on a soft romantic song, "What's New Pussy Cat" or "It's Now or Never." I stared into her eyes. When she started to blush I asked her to the dance floor. When she got closer, that was my signal. I said we really should be going home. She said the night is young, yes we should, your place or mine. So I took her to my place. I tried 'The English Patient' maneuver on her and presto we're in for the night. Can't say anymore because what we did was too damn vulgar and sweet, hahaha.

By the way, she brings me milk and cookies every day at 4 AM sharp for free, hahaha, I always reciprocate by tipping her, don't ask!!!

Last week I was doing some landscaping in my back yard when I accidentally hit a gold mine. I discovered oil, aka black gold. I was so excited, I called my boss and told him what he could do with my job. Yep, shove it where it doesn't shine. A week later I got a huge bill from my oil company that I owed them a ton of money. And here I am putting that gushing oil into them giant beer barrels (one hundred and forty to be exact). That's when I realized I didn't hit pay dirt, I cracked into their oil lines and now I got to beg my boss for forgiveness so I can get my job back. I'm so ashamed. But I know how to butter him up, take him out for lunch at the 'all you can eat sushi bar' and pop him the question. Might have to take him to the girlie bar too if I know him! That freaking horny toad. Needless to say, I got the job back but not before begging him for mercy. Thank you all.

Folks, I got a story to tell you that will knock your socks off. Today marks the 8th anniversary of the death of my fifth wife. See we were in a car accident and she died instantly. My arm was so badly hurt that they had to amputate it. Yep, it was hanging on its last nerve. So as they were harvesting all her organs I asked the doctor if they could do an arm transplant which would benefit me in two ways. I would get a new arm and at the same time she would be a part of me forever and a day. So after that forty-five minute, twenty-five doctor assisted operation it went off without a hitch. The only setback was that it would be a little shorter, five inches, a whole lot smoother like a baby's butt, and hairless like just back from a Brazilian waxing job. But who cares as long as I can do what I do. What do I do? I beat the meat silly in the back of Geraldo's Butcher Shop. I'm a prize fighter to be. A few months later on a follow up visit the doctor wanted to know how it was hanging. No not that. My arm you silly goose. And I said fine except I got one problem. Every time I go to pee, the hand won't let go. See I knew you weren't going to believe me no how, Jimmy laughs and bows!!!
(Play Roy Hamilton song "Don't Let Go")

The crowd hoots and hollers and gives him a standing ovation. Oh, you are all so kind. Let me tell you another story that you're just not going to believe. I read all the obituaries, and look for opportunities whenever the right moment arises. I make my way over to that dead person's home and pretend to be a long-lost lover or an abandoned son. It has to be somebody who has no children and no siblings. It makes it easier to get what I'm after, their money and belongings. I say we were lovers some 20-30 years ago and our only child, Juanito or Rosie, you pick the name, died at birth or she gave me up for adoption. I know it sounds crazy. Well if she's dead what good is her money and valuables? I might as well get some or all of it. Hey, do you know anybody who just died and was fully loaded? No, not that kind of loaded. What do you think I am? A pervert? Don't answer that. I do notice there's not too many prospective victims out there. It's all on account of the mortality rate going up. But at the same time, more folks are going senile, you know, suffering from dementia or Alzheimer's. So for those people I got to get to them when they're half crazy. Get them to like me, sign over powers of attorney to me and presto I clean house. Say no more, my lips are sealed!!!

Hey, you can add 'Insurance Con Man' to my distinguished resume, BAM!!!! And for your information, it was me who came up with that phrase first not Emeril Lagasse. He just copied me when we used to hang together. Well, never mind that. Let me tell you how I earned that title 'Insurance Con Man.' A few months ago the boys and I were playing poker. Oh we get together every weekend, drink some beers, watch the fights, and play for heavy stakes. Usually there are two or three hundred dollars riding on that table. Not bad for eight or nine players. I had noticed David Lennihan was a little bit stiff. So I asked him—what was wrong? He told me, he was in a car accident. While sitting in his car at a stop sign, he was struck from behind by a Cadillac driven by some guy named Jonathan Trump. So that's when Sally 'Salvatore' Bonanno says you're sitting on a goldmine. So that's when I chimed in, yep, and if you play your cards right, I can make you rich. You should have seen Lennihan's eyes light up. So he says, how's that? I say, what hit you, a Cadillac, who was driving it, a white rich man by the name of Trump. So I tell Lennihan I got an old neck brace thingy, a cane and a walker. Starting today and every day, I want you to use them. I'll get my lawyer, Alma Albright to represent you in a whiplash case. That babe is hot! No, not hot that way, hot that she never loses a case. But then, what do I know if she's hot in the sack, hahahaha. By the time we're finished with him, Jonathan Trump, we'll own one of the Trump buildings and it'll be 50, 25, and 25. So Lennihan says "I get the 50," and I say "No, I get the 50." Who came up with the scheme? Me, who's going to give you the neck brace, the cane, and the walker? Me, and then Lennihan says "Oh." Well folks, that's how my insurance con days started. So if you know somebody just recently hurt, send them my way and you'll get a finder's fee. How much? Thirty bucks! Hey, I'll keep you abreast of the case. The next time you hear from me, I'll be saying "I PARK MY CAR BY THE HARBOR." Yes, I will be rolling in the dough and girls galore, every which way I go. Farewell and it's Mr. Jimmy from here on now!!!

I got some exciting news to reveal. First of all I've never won a thing in my life. Well that goldfish in that little eight ounce bowl I won at the feast doesn't count. Plus, it died a week later. Don't remind me. You are looking at a lotto winner. You heard it right, a winner! I don't know what to do with myself. I got so many things I need. Converse sneakers, guess jeans, you know the ones with the embroidery all over it, a new toothbrush, a Stetson hat so when I entertain the folks in the streets I can pass it around and make a killing. And besides I'm tired of putting cardboard inside my shoe, it has a hole the size of a half a dollar. Hey, can you give me any suggestions? It's burning a hole in my pocket. I'm not telling any of my friends or family members. If my ex-mothers-in-law were to find out they'd be knocking on my doors and windows until I opened up. One's a creature from down under. That's another story I'll tell you some other time. Let's just say she has a spitting resemblance to Satan. So back to me. What should I do with my winnings? All 145 dollars and 32 cents? Hey, maybe Nicky Cannon can help a brother out. He looks like a giving man, and the way he dresses, you can tell he's loaded, money, money, money!!!
(Play The O'Jays song "For The Love Of Money")

Here's another of my revelations. I've decided I want to be a 'Cowboy'! Yep, I've been hanging out in those cowboy bars in New Jork City. We got two or three of them smack in the middle of Manhattan. In fact do you remember that Dolly Parton and Sylvester Stallone movie 'Rhinestone Cowboy'? It's one of them. And are you ready for this? I can spit like the rest of them and to look authentic and bona fide I'm learning to hoot and holler. I'm going to buy me a cowboy hat; I think they call them a Stetson, beret or some shit. I'm going to get me some spurs as well. What the heck, I need a change in my life. I've gotten too soft in the middle, and I hear them cowgirls are all that, and then some. That they kiss on a first date and . . . Well that's all I can say right here. But know, I'll be tall in the saddle. I'm practicing my John Wayne walk and my John Wayne talk. So if you don't hear from me any time soon Pilgrim, know I'll be packing my rags and heading somewhere out west. No, not New Jersey, farther out west, Texas or Alabama. Heck, that's why I'm learning how to do the hokey pokey. Those square dances are the real deal. No more Macarena or the Lambada for me. So long partner! Giddy up, happy trails until we meet again! See, already I sound like a cowboy, yaaaaaaaa hoooooooo.
(Jimmy bows down indicating he's finished)

That's my Stetson hat, I won it in a poker game. The guy who lost it told me it was once the property of John Wayne's. I wear it when I want to pick up babes and I diddy bop like the Duke. You just know nobody's going to mess with me. Gotta go Pilgrim, Corky's all saddled up and raring to go, Missy is awaiting!!!

The crowd begins to hoot and holler. Jimmy has made their day. They reward him by throwing money onto the stage. His manager runs up and collects every single dollar, two hundred and ninety-five in all, and a few wooden coins. But what the heck something is better than nothing. With the added money, Jimmy and his daughter book a room and take a breather. They eat, shower, and rest up. Jimmy invites one of the waitresses over for a few drinks and god knows what else. It lets him unwind before he goes on stage once more before departing the next day. Later Jimmy and Maggie, that's her name, that cute little waitress out of the UK he met earlier with the biggest brown eyes this side of heaven mosey on down to the bar, to socialize with the crowd and get to know each other a little better. She orders a Margarita and Jimmy a bottle of tequila. About an hour later this motorcycle guy diddy bops in like he owns the place. He is tore up from the floor up, and had earrings pierced all over his face. In his ears, nose, bottom lip, eyebrows and god knows where else. So he notices Jimmy staring at him and says to him what the f@#k he's looking at. So Jimmy nonchalantly downs that tequila drink in his hand, and proceeds to tell him, don't mind me. I was in the war, did a few tours just in Dessert Storm alone. I had to dodge bullets and hand grenades day in and day out. I had to have a drink to calm my nerves day in and day out. They say while

26

in one of my drinking binges, I got so drunk and I screwed a parrot. I thought maybe you might have been one of my offspring. So then Jimmy took a handful of his throat with his left hand, and that Dodo Bird went down. He begged daddy, that's Jimmy, for mercy. Jimmy then with his right hand grabs him by the seat of his pants, and throws him out the door, head first. End of story, Dodo Bird back on the extinction list, period.

Let me teach you something about cornbread. When I was up the river on my third visit I had to set a bunch of low-life mothers you know what, that you don't mess with Jim because if you let your guard down just once they will try to own you. I had to be tough and take no lip or shit from no one. The bigger they were the more I had to be crazy because that was my way out. If you want to earn respect you got to be crazy. No, I mean you got to look the part and play the part. The very first day this big ugly dude came up to me and wanted my cornbread. Well, that was the first and last time anybody wanted my cornbread. Because I shoved my size ten and a half shoe up his butt. Then while he was down, I kicked him some more and to this day he washes my clothes. So you see you got to act crazy when you're in a bind. Do what the crazy folks do: scream, holler, bite, scratch eyes out, rip noses and ears off. They will never ever bother you again. Yep, I'm crazier than a fox and Mike Tyson put together, you don't want to know! My middle name is terror, and that's a fact Jackass!!!

It's close to midnight and time for Jimmy to make his final appearance on the stage before heading back out on the road to Hollywood in the AM. Check out his stories below:

Folks, I'm going into the tabloid business as a 'News Reporter' where I reveal the dirt and rumors going around. I don't even have to interview anybody. Just pick a name, and presto I make him or her person of the hour. For example, I can say Charlie Sheen is dating a set of twin sisters. Yeah, he wants to keep it a family affair, hahaha. Pick another, John Mayer, good choice, I can say he's replacing Hugh Hefner, because the old one aint working like it used too. Heck, he's dating one gal, what happened to the three he was gallivanting with? And since Mayer is a rock star you know he's going to party like a rock star. Pee Wee Herman, oh, he's been rumored to play Dirty Harry, don't ask. But we can say he's good with his hands. I got plans to be bigger and better than Jerry Springer and Howard Stern put together. It's going to be racy and trashy yet classy. I might even win a Pulitzer Prize or a Grammy. Just you wait and see.

Hey, this question is for the ladies out there. Have you ever had a spat with your lover boy and then realized you were wrong? Well, that's what happened to me. She tried every trick in the book from sending me flowers, a bottle of the finest wine, a cologne and all with intents to reconcile. But what really did the trick was when she came over to my crib all wrapped up in her trench coat. When she came inside the door and took it off, she didn't have a stitch of clothing underneath. Oh lordie lord! Good god in heaven! Is this woman sweet! How I know? I had a mouthful, hahaha, don't ask, I said a mouthful!!!

Folks, I got a story that will amaze you like it always does to me. Talk about hanging on to your bloomers and toupees. Well this will blow them away. I was in an Irish pub with my Irish friend, Mickey J. Yeah, that nut who introduced me to a lot of crazy ideas. He was looking depressed. So I asked him, "Why the gloomy face?" He told me he just heard an old flame of his had died. So I asked him, "How long ago?" He replied, "Two weeks ago." So I jumped out of my seat after drinking a glass of tequila, and we ran home to get two shovels. He wanted to know what for? I said, "So we can excavate her remains up." So, he looks at me and says, "Did you hear what I said?" "She's dead!" I said, "Yeah, but if you want to keep her alive, we can taxidermy her body." He said, "What do you mean, she's deader than a door nail." So I sat him down and explained what I was planning to do if any of my lover girls die. Stuff them up and mount their bodies on the wall, like those game hunters do. We're not just going to put her head up there but the whole body. Plus, I can't bear cutting her head off. That's too gruesome! So he asked me, "What I'm going to do with her body?" So I smiled and said, "When you freaking get that urge, you mount her!" "You climb up a ladder, and have your way with it." He smiled and gave me a great big ole bear hug that almost knocked the wind out of me. Now tell me I aint smart! Brighter than a light bulb, that's for sure! So we rushed over to the graveyard, and dug her up. Well, this is why I said, "Hang on to your bloomers and toupees!" Her body was partially wormed up. You know decayed. So I said, "Oh well, there goes your urges! It's too late but if you want a souvenir that's all you can have." Hey, you should see what I took, don't ask! It's in my freezer next to the other chicken breasts. He took a piece of her heart. Now tell me I aint good for something. Hey, you got a loved one? I suggest you get them to sign a prenuptial agreement. That way you can satisfy your urges, byeeee!!!
(Play Janis Joplin song "A Piece of My Heart")

Here's one for the road. About five years ago, I had some problems with my baby. So I went to my fortune teller. After reading my palm, she said, "Jimmy, what you need is a love potion to kick start your mojo." I yelled out, "What the heck is a mojo?" She looked me in the eye and said, "When you need a little help to arouse your—you know what!" It's made from an ingredient they use to make Viagra." So I took a swig. Omg, that stuff is nasty! I told her, "What you trying to do to me? Kill me!" I stormed out of

there upset. When I got home my so and so was stiff as a rock. I proceeded to call my woman, told her I had a present for her and to hurry right on over. When she walked in I immediately grabbed her and . . . , and then . . . Well let's just say our love life has never been the same since. And get this, I drove her all the way home and that's without leaving the apartment. So if you know anybody having problems, tell them to visit that gypsy on 45th and Vine. Tell them Jimmy sent ya!!!
(Play The Clovers song "Love Potion No. 9")

The owner of the club was smiling, well pleased with Jimmy's performance, thanked him profusely and tells him he is more than welcomed to come back anytime he's in town. Maggie exchanges addresses and phone numbers with Jimmy. They kiss goodbye because she's got another shift to do before going home to her mom's house on the other side of town. Jimmy goes up to his room, and sacks out for the next five hours. He wakes up at 6 AM, alerts his daughter that it's time to pack, and be on the road. They have breakfast at a local restaurant, a block away, and finally get back on the road by 7:30 AM.

After driving for almost eight hours they negotiate a one night stand of two performances. One at 7:30 PM, the other at 10:30 PM at a popular casino called 'The Primrose Lane.' He books two rooms, eats dinner, showers, and rests up before he has to go on stage. His daughter does some sight-seeing, window shopping, always looking for a bargain. She still has close to a hundred dollars out of her share and spends it wisely. Jimmy goes through his material to choose which jokes to use. He arrives early to the stage to ensure the sound system is working properly. He's more than eager to start which will be in a matter of seconds. The MC introduces Jimmy:

Folks, I got a story to tell you about my very first encounter with the law. It's all on account of me wanting to get a screw. Let me start from the beginning. I'm a dabbler. I dabble a bit here and a bit there. No, not the stock market! Are you crazy? I just like to tinkle. You know open up things and probe with my hands and eyes. I was having trouble with my tellie. What's a tellie? That's what the folks from the UK call a television. I see you haven't seen any of those British programs like Mrs. Brown or Sherlock Holmes. Well in the UK that word is used all the time. Back then, a television consisted of tubes, screws, nuts and bolts. So by dabbling, I was able to get the television going like brand new, except I needed a screw or two. So I ran to the mall, and bumped into this dapper looking fellow. I asked him if he knew where I could get a screw. He said at the penthouse, on the top of the mall. I worked my way to the elevator. The elevator man asked me, "What floor?" So I said, "To the penthouse." Then he said, "Are you sure?" And I said, "Where else can I get a screw?" So then he said, "You've come to the right place!" So we reach the top. This palooka-looking, thug greets me and asks me what I wanted. So I said, "A screw or two." Then he asked me, "The two hundred dollar model?" I said, "No!" Then he said, "The hundred and fifty dollar one?" I said, "No!" Then he said, "The fifty dollar piece?" I said, "No, no that's still too high!" So he asked me, "Well how much are you willing to spend?" I replied, "Two cents!" Then with a smirk on his face, he opened up a door and yelled out, "Hey Mac, bring up the old cat!" Just as he uttered those words, in rushed fifteen S.W.A.T. cops. They told us we're all under arrest for prostitution. Before I could say another word, they chained us up together, brought us to a paddy wagon, and drove us to the courthouse. Twelve half-naked girls, two goons, and this well-dressed dude who looked like a lady (who I surmised was the ringleader), and me. By this time, I was pleading with the lieutenant that I was only looking for a screw. Then he said, "That's why you're here." So we're all thrown into a big holding cell with a bunch of other low-lifers, mother rapers, father rapers, pick-pocketers, and god knows what else. So here I am innocent and mingling with a bunch of crooks. A few of the girls took notice of me, winking and showing me their boobs. But by this time, all I had on my mind was how was I going to get out of there. When it was my turn to make that one call, I called my mama. She said she was going to ring my neck. I told her, I was just dabbling. The ringleader who was eavesdropping on my call, asked me if I was into the stock markets. I said to him, "I don't affiliate myself with thugs and crooks." Then he gave me a dirty look. I just moved away from him. It took me three days to prove my innocence. But in the meantime, my face was splattered all over town. Now I'm a persona non grata. To make matters worse, I lost my job, and got kicked out of school. But on the bright side, I have a date with Sally. She's one of the escort girls. She was only in the business for two days, so that doesn't count. Omg, you should see her! Voluptuous and hot, is all I can say. I can't wait till I bring her home to meet mama. Well maybe not. Moral of the story—when you dabble, be careful when you need a screw, because you might get screwed at the end.

By the way, when that incident occurred my real name was Dick Hurts. My face was plastered in every newspaper in town, and featured on every news channel on TV. My family name was mud. My mother was telling everybody I was an adopted son. My sisters all changed their names because they too didn't want to be associated with me. And that judge who threw the book at me thought since I was there for two screws, I was planning one of them there three-way ménage a thingy. Hey, they can all believe what they want! All I know was that I needed to get two screws. So I had my lawyer change my name. In fact, this incident did me a favor. Who wants to be called Dick Hurts? In school, I was the butt of everybody's jokes. They would say, "How's Tricky Dicky?" or "Here comes Big Dick!" or "Show me what you got big boy!" and the girls called me "Hammer on the block!" So now I get no flack. I still sign my name Dick Hurts, but that's because I am what I am. No Tom, Dick, or Harry is going to change that! Thanks for hearing me out.

Folks, I got another story I want to tell you. But you fellas better hold onto your toupees, and you girls better tie a knot onto your bloomers because this will blow them away. My grandfather was a wee bit crazy, a drunk or both because he did the unthinkable. He committed suicide. How? Good question! He shot himself directly underneath his left breast. When my grandmother got wind of this, she was so depressed that she decided she had to join that old fool. So the very next day she asked me to fetch her gun. Me, I was too young to realize what she was up to. So I did as she asked. Then she told me to "Go Now!" As I walked out the door, I heard a bang or a bing. Don't recall exactly but I think it was more like a thump. See she tried to do what my grandfather had done. She shot directly under her left breast. We had to rush her to the hospital. She shot her kneecap. Now she rides one of them there electric wheel chairs. You should see her pop wheelies! Evel Knievel would be proud of her. I know I am!!!
(Play The Zombies song "Go Now")

I've been getting a lot of invitations to those dating sites through the internet. Why last week I got 'Meet Jewish Girls,' 'Arabian Girls,' 'Russian Girls,' 'Hot Latinas,' 'Scrumptious Irish Girls,' 'Irresistible Italian Girls,' 'Sexy Scottish Babes.' I paid a visit to my fortune teller and without me saying a word she said I was going to meet a whole slew of women. But the only way that was going to happen, is if I joined those web sites. What do I got to lose? They ask personal questions, like am I interested in easy girls, or them hard to get ones. What a dumb question! Easy ones of course! Then they ask if sex is my priority or just meeting intellectual sophisticated women? I don't know where they get these questions. Any moron would know the answer to that is—sex! Can't get none! That's why I'm here to get more than I can chew, hahaha! Pardon the pun! Then they want to know nationality, color skin, color hair, color eyes, tall or short, and if measurement is a key factor. Good god! The only thing important to me is that they don't have what I got, or blind, or in a wheel chair. Otherwise any ole woman will do! Beggars can't be choosey! But I do want something to grab on to when we get down. You ever see them movies, where two lovers are ripping off each other's clothes? Well that's what I seek. One hot, feisty woman to knock my socks off, make me scream, holler and bend for her. Let me put it another way. I'm a hunk who's dying to climb Mt. Everest. She has to be easy, fun loving, willing to venture to the unknown, take me to heights I've never been to, and show me what she has from top to bottom. If you know anybody like that, send her my way. I will pamper her . . .

In Hollywood the competition starts out with close to one thousand entries, and it'll take at least three days to make the cuts. On the second day, Jimmy goes on stage and passes to the next round for his trip back to the Big Apple. But not before he tells them a few jokes. Check them out below:

Folks, I think you already heard by now that my friend Felix Baumgartner made that death defying twenty-four mile sky dive jump from outer space. Well, it was my idea. I had planned to do that historic jump first. But somebody stole my parachute, and he beat me to the punch. Well, I'm going to do one better. I'm going to go to our nearest planet. I think its Mercury. I know it starts with an M, but not Mars. It's definitely Mercury. And I plan to jump from there to earth. I know it's going to take me a few weeks to get here. Maybe even longer. But then I'm going to own that record, and leave Felix in the dust. So wish me luck! When I get back, I expect a parade, and lots of women at my doorstep. And yes, this is another one to bite the dust from my bucket list. I'm going to be bigger than Paul McCartney, Ellen DeGeneres, Clint Eastwood, and Oprah Winfrey, all put together. Yes, that Oprah! Have you ever heard of 'The Color Purple?' Yep, that one! The one that smacked Harpo in the kisser! There's no end to my madness. See you when I get back. I'll be the Guinness Record Holder just yet, ooooooooooo ooooooooooo ooooooooooo!!!

As most of you don't know, I'm an entrepreneur waiting to happen. I just filed a patent for my latest invention. Let me start from the beginning. When you go to the beach, lake, or a public pool what do you notice about the men? They are becoming top heavy. Yeah, I know it's not a pretty sight. So I've invented a man bra. Don't laugh but it is true! I'm also developing a one piece suit. Yep, just like the girls wear. Maybe even a two piece would be popular. I'm going to Brazil next week to try it out. Can you all see me now with a thong and a hooters bra? Yeah, I'm starting to have breasts, and they are starting to sag. So if anybody has any ideas of trying to steal my invention they can fuhgettaboudit. I've filed a utility patent. Omg, I'm going to look pretty when I hit the beaches, I'll be singing "I'm so pretty, very pretty." Might get sexy and daring and take it all off. Well over there it's the norm. I'll be frolicking on the beach and those girls will be frolicking with me. I might as well stay there and ride on a float with all those sexy girls when the Carnival comes into town. Oh, you'll recognize me aright. I'll be the one jumping up and down, dressed in all hot pink outfits, mask, thong, and my new invention, Jimmy's Man Bra. Hey, if any of you want to join me, come along! Please bring your thongs and your skimpy bras. We'll be the drop dead gorgeous folks from da Eu Es of Aye. Now I know what they mean when a girl says to another girl, "How's It Hanging?" Don't ask, bye, bye!!!

Here's a story I never told anybody. I was driving on the expressway on my way to work a few weeks back when this fire department emergency truck cut in front of me, almost pushing me off the road. Oh, I was fuming mad! About a quarter mile down the road, its back doors opened up, and out came flying this US Postal box. So as I neared the box, I slowed down. Curious me had to see what was inside of it, and why the hurry. So I pushed it to the side of the road, and proceeded to open it up. It was a box of toes, all covered with ice. No, really, toes. It was probably bound for a skin graft operation or maybe some toe transplants. I never heard of that procedure but what do I know? So I whipped out my cell phone and proceeded to call a 'tow truck.' Hey, hope your day was exciting as mine! Have a good one!!

That's an ambulance similar to the one that almost drove me off the road. And that's the box of toes that fell out of its back doors. Now I know why it was in such a hurry, it was on its way for some kind of surgery. Never heard of a toe transplant but what do I know, maybe to be used as skin graft!!!

 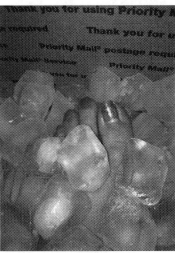

Here's an incredible story I hope won't alarm you. I was on my way to work a few days ago when I hopped on a NYC bus. It was crowded as always but I did manage to find me a seat next to this man who appeared to be drunk. At the same time, he was all dressed up and wearing a ton of bling, bling. You know jewelry including: rings, watches, bracelets, earrings, and chains all over his body. And to top it off, he had his arm leaning outside the window ledge acting like Mr. Cool. After a few stops, the bus proceeded to make a 90 degree turn to the left. As we were doing that, a truck was making a 90 degree turn into the right lane, when they collided. The man's arm was amputated or as some would say decapitated, same shit! There was blood and guts all over the place, even on my clothes. Mama will be whipping me good tonight. She aint going to believe this story, no how! Heck, if I wasn't there, I wouldn't believe it myself. All I can say it was a gruesome sight. Joseppi, the bus driver, immediately pulled to the right, and had all the passengers get off the bus to wait for the next available one. Joseppi waited for an ambulance to escort the man to the nearest hospital. Two boys who were on the bus located the man's arm and removed most of the jewelry. They were having difficulty removing two of the rings. So they picked up the arm and ran down the street with it. It was like a scene from out of a Looney Tunes cartoon. A cop car shortly made its way to the scene. We immediately informed them of the boys' actions. The police quickly gave chase. They apprehended the kids three blocks away, and handcuffed them. We were later informed that the kids were being charged with, get this, 'armed robbery.' Thank god there's a cop when you need one! Only proves they're not all sleeping or munching away on some donuts in an alley way somewhere. Well, have a good day, and don't take any wooden nickels!

That's the NYC bus that was involved in that accident, poor man never knew what hit him. By the way, I got one of his earrings. Well I earned it, he ruined my new shirt and pants with all that body matter, ugggh you don't want to know. I wear it when I go bowling or bar hopping looking to meet hot mamas. Damn, don't I look good even if I say so myself!!!

Folks, I don't know about you but many of my buddies are presently divorced. I noticed they all had one thing in common. They all married a pretty woman. Now I have a friend named Giacomo who married an ugly chick. They are the only couple still happily married to this day. Giacomo figured that if he married an ugly woman, he would be happy forever and a day. For one thing, she'll always prepare his meals, and give him

peace of mind that nobody's going to hit up on her. They have been happily married now for over thirty some odd years. My question to you is, "Would you marry a good looking soul-mate who has the tendency to flirt, or would you marry an ugly woman/man?" Me personally, and I hope you take it from "my personal point of view"—I would look to see what's in her purse first, and then make up my mind. Yesiree Bob! Show me the money! Money talks. Nobody walks! I was born at night, but not last night!!!
(Play Jimmy Soul song "If You Wanna Be Happy")

Hey folks, I got a story to tell and I hope you don't get insulted, especially if you're a mother or think I'm talking about your mama but what I am about to tell you might upset you. Remember that story about that fortune I won in the lotto. Yeah, all $115.93, well that lowdown good for nothing mother-in-law of mine tried to get a piece of the pie as I suspected. Thank the lord she's no longer related to me because her daughter and I are divorced but she's still the grandmother to my kids. She had the audacity to ask me to lend her eighty-five dollars. She said her cat died. She needed another cat to prevent termite problems. Heck! More than likely, she will go find a cat in the street and tell me she bought it. You don't know that lady like I know that lady. She just wants to buy some more wine, Thunderbird or Captain Jack. That old wino! And yes, she does look like Satan or his mother because she's one ugly mother. When I was dating her daughter back in the day, she was so sweet and kind. Yeah, she would butter me up, so I would marry her daughter. That cheap so and so! After we got married, I made a vow never to see Aluisa ever again. However her house burned down (an arson job no doubt). She stayed with us for nine months. It was the longest grueling nine months in my life. She's so nosy and had to know everything, like when I got home on paydays. Sure as the moon rises she wanted to know how much I made. She would be eavesdropping whenever her daughter and I were making whoopee. Knowing her, she probably wanted to get in on the action, that horney toad. Come to think of it. I noticed how she kept looking at me. But Oooooh, I just wanted to kill her. I threw the biggest going-away party when she left my home. Hey fellas, do yourself a favor, if ever your mother-in-law wishes to move into your home, dig a ditch and throw yourself in it. It will save you the agony. That's all I got to say!
(Play Roy Hamilton song "You Can Have Her")

A lot of people ask me what I do for a living. Well, prior to writing Rock 'N Roll trivia books, I was a 'Hit Man.' Yes, a killer for money! But I rather not talk about this here. I also did time in the pokey before that, for trying to rob a bank. You won't believe this but my grandmother was my getaway driver. We got caught on our first and only robbery attempt. She fell asleep at the wheel. So for any of you thinking of robbing banks, get yourself a good getaway driver. I got eleven years, and grandma got two months. She should have gotten those eleven years. Heck! She's the one who raised me. While in prison, I learned the trade very well. I can kill a person with just one bite. I can get out of hand cuffs, and use all types of weapons. I'm a master of Three Card Monte. I can woo ladies out of all their savings because I'm a lover-man. No, I love girls, not men! So that's it in a nut shell. And yes, I'm available, call me Suga! No, my name is Jimmy, you're Suga!!!

Hey, you're not going to believe this but I see dead people just like the kid in *The Sixth Sense* (from that Bruce Willis movie). And not just any ordinary dead people, but people in their birthday suits. Yes, you heard it right! Naked like a jay bird. I don't know if this is a curse or a blessing. I'm going to see my fortune teller, and see what she thinks. That woman is smarter than a jackass and a hound dog put together. The last time I saw that gypsy woman, she tried to set me up on a blind date with her sister. That girl was one ugly mother, you know what? She had tattoos all over her body, including her butt. Oooooh, you don't want to know. So what do you suggest I do? Go see a shrink or go to my fortune teller? Let me know what you recommend. Write me here, care of my good friend Nick Cannon, and send me some dough, I'll pray for you, thanks!!!

I have a story, or should I say, a confession to reveal. When I was a kid of seventeen I was seduced by a woman nearly twice my age. She was so infatuated with me, but I did not see it coming. She asked me to come over to her house to do a paint job. And I aint talking toe nails. She said to arrive after midnight. I wondered, why so late? It didn't dawn on me but as we were removing all the furniture she saved the bed for last. That too kind of surprised me. It should have been a red flag. Then she brought me a plateful of exotic foods, clams, mussels, shrimp, lobsters, caviar, and crab meat. She said, "You deserve a bonus!" Then she brought in two glasses, and a bottle of red wine. She put on the stereo, and had The Delfonics singing all their greatest hits. Woo, I love The Delfonics! As we chatted, she kept pouring me more and more wine. Shortly after, I was starting to feel a bit woozy. So I had to lay down a bit. Before I knew it, she came into the room buck naked. Omg, I then realized what she was up to. But by then, I was helpless as a kitten. She had her way with me. Moral of the story is never work after midnight or trust a woman who likes The Delfonics songs. She will more than likely blow your mind, hahaha!
(Play The Delfonics song "Didn't I (Blow Your Mind This Time")

Ladies and gentlemen, are you aware that John Wayne, America's greatest action-packed hero, is responsible for two important things? How's that? Well, when Buddy Holly was writing one of his songs, he was stuck with the lyrics. But while watching the movie, 'The Searchers' he took John's words from a scene and incorporated it into the song, "That'll Be The Day." What's the other thing? John said, "Corky we're saddling up. We're going south of the border to please Missy." Now you know why you girls get so excited when we guys say those words. It's going to be one heck of a ride or should I say feast, hahaha!!!

Folks, are you familiar with the singing sensation, The Honey Cone? Well they had a major hit in 1971 with the song, *Want Ads,* which would climb to the top of the charts. Well, that's me to a 't', single and free. And if you want some it's yours for the taking, because I will more than tickle your fancy. Want to know more? Experienced is what I am. So if you got what I don't have, then call me, and bring me some sugar. While we're at it, lots of spending loot will also do the trick! Did I say trick? Girl I will give you lots of trick or treats. It isn't Halloween but then again it could be. What is it that you want me to do? Hey, this is a family show! Don't be talking nasty! But then again, I can get good and nasty as you want me to, hahaha. You see I've been around the block more times than you can count! Shoot, the last time I had a fling with a gal, I think she's still in never, never land and doesn't want to come down. So check me out, and also The Honey Cone, ciao and how!!!
(Play The Honey Cone song "Want Ads")

I got some bad news and some good news to tell you. Recently, I took my girl to a fancy restaurant. As we were eating, she noticed a roach stuck to an ice cube in her drink. She almost fainted. When I pointed it out to the waiter, he immediately reported it to the owner of the establishment. They told us the dinner and any more drinks was on the house, and that we could come again for another free meal any time soon. So that's the bad news. Now get ready for the good news. I'm going to scheme restaurants out of free meals. How's that you ask? I'm asking my friend Guillermo to get me some roaches. Well, I aint got any roaches. But Guillermo has everything! What he aint got, he can get dead or alive. I'll throw him a few bucks, two or three. Two is more like it, for his troubles. I'll be going to the finest restaurants and bringing the roaches, again and again. I will be partying and eating like the rock star that I am, hahaha. Hey, keep this to yourself! I don't need anyone to ruin this game plan of mine, hahaha. I will be packing on weight galore. My 155 pound frame will turn into a massive 200 pounder, in no time. Hey, maybe you want to give it a try. You might just like it, and remember who told you about it! Me!!!

Folks, I was scamming restaurants for a free meal by planting roaches in the food they were serving us. I got away with it twenty times. But here's what happened on my twenty-first attempt. I took my girl and four of our best friends to a fancy restaurant in NYC. We ordered the best, and two bottles of Dom Pérignon. We were having a swell time, dancing, eating, drinking, and laughing when all of a sudden the roaches in that match box came lose in my suit jacket. All twelve of them went lose as I was dancing. The critters were crawling all over me. I was itching like a bug. I started to dance the jitterbug in hopes they would all come out. The folks at the tables were starting to clap for me. I guess I was dancing up a storm. They thought I must have been Fred Astaire or Michael Jackson reincarnated. My girl was so surprised and unable to catch up with me. She looked so happy for me. But then I whispered in her ear about the roaches. She jumped back and started to laugh uncontrollably, but from a distance. Then I noticed the roaches were falling to the ground. So I did my Sammy Davis Jr. tap dance routine only to stomp them critters to death. I was smoking hot with my tap dancing. I did manage to kill all but one. When the owner heard and saw my performance, the folks started clapping and giving me a standing ovation. The owner took the bill, tore it up, saying "You should come again!" Well, I did achieve my goal, a free meal. The moral of the story is let somebody else hold the roaches. Two or three roaches should be more than enough. A dozen roaches is way too much!

(Play Leo Sayer song "Long Tall Glasses")

Ladies and gentlemen I got some incredible news to reveal. I was a pole dancer back in the day. I could do spins, somersaults, and cartwheels right there up in mid-air. I was so committed that, in Vegas, I competed for the title of 'Mr. Pole Dancer USA'. But sad to say, I came in dead last. I know I shouldn't give up. Heck, where we would be if Christopher Columbus made a 180 degree turn back? We'd still be in England saluting King George the 23rd. Well, anyway as I was doing my fifteen minute presentation, I had a wardrobe malfunction. My package came out. Yep, nuts and all, don't remind me! I just wanted to die. I got to look at the bright side, I bonded with a whole slew of girls. They liked what they saw. No, not that, my performance, and then again maybe it was that after all. I guess when you got it, like I got it everybody wants it. Hey, do me a favor, don't tell anybody about my wardrobe malfunction. I would be the laughing stock in TV. All the talk shows, will be ripping me apart for weeks, and maybe even months. I can see it now, Letterman, Leno, Kimmel, Fallon, Daly, Conan, Arsenio, Harvey, Lopez, and not to mention The View, The Talk, Kelly and Michael, Wendy, Ellen, Bethenny, and that lawyer guy from TMZ. I have to admit that was not my proudest moment. Let's not ever mention this again!!!

Folks, I have this urge to jump back on the saddle. No not that, I mean the pole. Earlier today I told you how I came in last in the 'Mr. Pole Dancer 2013' competition in Vegas,

all on account of my package coming out. I had a wardrobe malfunction that ruined my chances of winning the title, and getting my name up in lights in Vegas. And you know what happens in Vegas is supposed to stay in Vegas. Except they blasted that sexy picture of me smack dab on the cover of every Vegas newspaper in town, and on every TV station. But anybody who knows me, knows failure is not an option in my book. So I'm giving it one more shot. I'll be bigger and better. Besides that, don't remind me. Ciao got to go practice, take care . . .
(Play Alabama song "Give Me One More Shot")

Folks, do you know why I have a successful track record as a love man? It's because I have the ability to wrap my body around a woman's torso. Why's that? I'm a contortionist, you know double-jointed in eight different locations. Sometimes I get so tied up that I have to wait a while for certain body parts of mine to shrivel up. That can take at least an hour or two. That's a pain that hurts so good, don't ask. Well, that's why they love me! I can come from out of nowhere, and yes you don't want to know. See we interlock at certain places. It's an experience and feeling most women never had the pleasure of feeling. Unless they were lucky to be stuck to me, hahaha. In fact, have you ever heard that song by the Spinners "The Rubberband Man?" Who do you think gave them the inspiration for that song? Yep, yours truly! Check it out, and every time you hear that song think of me all tied up . . .
(Play the Spinners song "The Rubberband Man")

Folks, did I tell you I'm a 'Gun For Hire?' Don't let the size fool you? You got an ex-lover, a cheating boyfriend, girlfriend, a wife, a boss, a lawyer, a doctor, or a mother-in-law you want out of your misery? Well I'm your man! And I don't come cheap. I do a good job. You won't be incriminated. I can do it the quick and easy way so they won't know what hit them. Like in an explosion where they will suffer no pain. I'll rip their finger and toe nails off with a set of pliers. Then feed them to the crocodiles somewhere in Pottawattamie. Or I can drop them from an airplane. Believe me, it's quick and fatal. They'll have a heart attack before they even hit the ground. So tell me, how do you want it done? And it's all cash, no IOU's. And get this, for two or more death wishes, I'll give you a discount. Tell all your friends about me. All referrals will be compensated if a kill is generated. You get 10%. See ya! Remember to call me by the code name Kemosabe. You will be referred to as Tonto and like Leonard Cohen "I'm Your Man!!!"
(Play Leonard Cohen song "I'm Your Man")

Can I tell you a secret? I'm a natural born 'Scam Artist.' I pretend to be a long-lost orphan. When I find a prospective sucker I tell them I hired a private dick to find the parents who abandoned me at birth. How's it going? Well, so far I haven't had any luck. One time I told this lady that she was my mother. She died right there and then. Didn't even give me a chance to have her sign all the papers necessary to inherit her estate. Oh well, I'll keep trying till I succeed. You know what PT Barnum once said, "There's a sucker born every minute!" Now if I could only locate a handful, I'd be in the money. Hey, do you know any? I can cut you in on the deal. How does 10% sound to you? Ok, ok 12%. Take it or leave it. My daddy once said 12 of something is better than 12 of nothing. Keep me posted and mums the word! Don't need anybody cutting in on my brilliant idea. Hey, please excuse me. I got to read today's obituaries. There's been a rise in deaths this week. Must be those processed foods that those big food corporations are putting out . . .

I got a story to tell you. When I was thirteen, I fell in love with my homeroom teacher, Ms. Leib. I would get up early, brush my teeth, take a shower, comb my hair, put on some underwear I found in the hamper, and slap on some of my daddy's Old Spice aftershave lotion. No, I didn't have any hair to talk about. Heck, I didn't have any on my jimmy boy either! Maybe some fuzz but you'd need a magnifying glass to see that. If you want to know the truth, I was a late bloomer. But let's not talk about that here. Let's just say, I was special. Yeah, that's right, special! I even wore a football helmet to sleep (still do). So off to school I would go, and I would pass by the fruit store to swipe an apple for Ms. Leib. But what I really wanted was a watermelon. But can you see me now trying to stick that watermelon under my shirt, and the rest of me skinny as a long neck goose. Any way I would put that apple on her desk. There I am smiling from ear to ear with my hands crossed on top of my desk. Omg, I dreamed of her. You don't want to know, hahaha. What became of her? She's a pole dancer in some strip joint, getting tips, don't ask. The cold cash ones you freaking idiots. Hey, check out the song "Mr. Lee" by The Bobbettes and imagine it being about my woman Ms. Leib.

Hey, can you keep a secret? I found out where Ms. Leib pole dances. I'm always sitting up front. I hoot and holler the loudest. I give her plenty of tips. That's a no brainer. I'm her number one fan, ooooooooooooo ooooooooooooo ooooooooooooo!!!
(Play The Bobbettes song "Mr. Lee")

I got a question for you. Have you ever won anything in your life? Well, for me nothing to really talk about. In fact the only two times I ever won a thing was when I threw a quarter into a fish bowl. I won just that, a gold fish worth ten and a half cents after spending twenty-five dollars to win it. The booth attendant must have noticed me crying, and put that quarter into the bowl because she felt sorry for me. When she told me I had won, I nearly fainted. The second time I won a jackpot in bingo. But so did twenty-four other folks. So I had to split that 500 dollar prize with each person receiving twenty dollars. See, I have no luck! But I know my luck is about to change, and when it does you won't see, nor hear from me ever again. I'm getting me a piece of the pie in the sky. I will be taking a round trip around the world. I may start with a visit to the French Riviera. They say the ladies there are the most. And I will be riding high on that float when the Carnival comes around. I will be wearing a thong and a face mask, so you won't know it's me. Then I plan to hop over to the UK, wherever that is. I think it's in the Caribbean somewhere. Then Hawaii, the Polynesian Islands, and Vegas is a must! After all, what happens in Vegas stays in Vegas! You don't want to know. I'm a hunk! Well take my word. That's what I am, hunky-dory at that. Look at it this way, who do kings hang with? No, besides hookers, other kings. Who do the rich rub shoulders with? No, besides girl escorts, other rich people. So I being a hunk, I'm going to hang with hookers and girl escorts. No, you won't catch me with other hunks because I'm a straight man. I want to be with the hotties who have the bodies that don't have what I have. Ok, wish me luck and say a prayer for me, ciao . . .

Folks, there's another thing I want to tell you. I would appreciate if you keep it under wraps because it's not something you would be proud to brag about, especially in front of your kids. I'm a 'Junk Collector'. I go out at night scavenging for junk. You have no idea the money folks put out on the curbs, day in and day out. I have my steady route. I go to those rich neighborhoods, and score like a bandit. But I must warn you there are setbacks. I found this old piano. I had to hire six guys to load it onto my truck. When we got it to my home, one of the guys dropped his end, and a thousand roaches popped out of nowhere. I had those guys stomping them. At first they hesitated but when I mentioned a bonus, you should have seen them jumping up and down. Can you picture us doing the cucaracha mambo? We killed most of them, but every now and then a new colony pops up. My house stinks of roach spray. I can taste it in my mouth, ooooooh, don't ask. So if you're thinking of going into the junk business, take it from me, don't bring any garbage a hundred feet of your home. Or else, prepare to pay the price until you move away or die!!!

Folks, can you keep a secret? I got a vice I'm not too proud of. I'm a junkie. Yep, hard to the core, a "Junk Food Junkie" that is! I devour bags of chips, ho ho's, Twinkies, and ding dongs. But that's just for starters. Whoppers and big mac's aint safe with me because whatever I can't eat right there and then, I eat with my eyes. Chewing is my expertise! But sometimes I don't bother to chew. I just swallow. I swallow anything in sight. You would do it too, if you could. My favorite hang outs are at McDonalds, Burger Kings, Papa Johns, Denny's, Popeye's, Roy Rogers, KFC's, Red Lobster's, Applebee's, Dominoes, Good Eats, and Eat At Joe's. Well, pardon me but I got a date at the 'All You Can Eat Sushi Bar.' Don't wait up, I've been known to stay there for hours on end on my junk food binges. Got to go! I'm so hungry I can eat a horse and you too, hahaha. (Play Larry Groce song "Junk Food Junkie")

That's my favorite place right after home. It's just a skip and a hop from my man cave. Their cheeseburgers and gyros are finger licking good! And the food prices are just right. Big John, the proprietor, is so hospitable and so down to earth. His crew is the best. But don't just take my word. Come in, order some food and you too will agree that 'Good Eats,' is the best eatery in town. They are an A+ all the way!!!

Folks, I have to come clean. I am a 'Male Model.' Yep, I sit in the buff at art galleries, museums, art classes, and women's hen parties. You heard it right girls, in the nude! And may I say, I look hot and delicious, even if I say so myself, hahaha. The good part is, I can be had, just show me the money. So tell all your friends, sisters, mothers, and aunts that I can be theirs too. By the way, I don't come cheap or easy! But with a hunk like me, you get your monies worth! Call me, 24/7. I charge time and a half for after hours, and double time for holidays! Ciao baby! Hope to show you my stuff, hahaha, byeeeeeee . . .

I got a question to ask of you. Is it proper to tell a lady that you just met, "I'll paint your toe nails, and you paint my toe nails, and then we paint up the town red?" My daughter thinks that's sexual harassment. Heck, she's just jealous because my toe nails keep changing every week. They make me look gorgeous! Hahaha. Last week, a girl I met at Victoria's Secret chose hot pink. Therefore my toe nails are looking hot. But then maybe it was better when the previous gal had painted them orange. Well, you tell me. Is it ok to ask a girl that question? It always works for me. We end up with a nightcap and, and . . . well, use your imagination. Ok, ok, making love the whole night through and every so often come up for some air in between. Oh, you don't want to know, hahaha. Hey, have yourselves a wonderful day! If a stranger should come up to you, and asks you about painting your toes nails—don't be surprised, it might be me!!!

Btw, I'm thinking of opening up an escort business to go. I can escort you anywhere, and anytime. It could be your house, my house, up on the roof, or in your kitchen. Hey, there's no limit! But I do charge extra for nightcaps. You know that's when the juices are flowing, and you want to take it up a notch. So you post that 'Do Not Disturb! Gone Fishing' sign, outside your door knob and you lower the shades. Well, you get the idea. Call me Suga!!!

Folks, I'm looking for a few good men, ok, and women too. See, I'm going into the 'Kidnapper of Pets' for ransom business. Last week while I was strolling around the neighborhood. I saw a bunch of signs posted on the trees asking if anybody had seen this dog. That's when it hit me. I could hijack a pet for money. You know, like a car jack or an airplane hijack. Well it's the same thing except you grab a cat, dog, or bird. Heck, even a monkey if that's what they got! Then wait for the reward signs to go up. Now how do you price the ransom? That's an easy one. If there are a lot of signs up then that means the owner wants that pet back desperately. Now if too few signs go up, then that tells me they are not too concerned. Maybe a child in the household is the only one who wants the pet back. The parents don't care because it's just another mouth to feed, that they can do without. They put up the signs to make the child feel they are doing their best to get the pet back. But we know the real deal. So if you want to apply for the position, let me know.

Btw, does anybody know where Lassie lives? That would be a goldmine, if you catch my drift . . .

Folks, to jump start my 'Kidnapper of Pets' for ransom business, and to test the waters, I've posted a picture of my cat Pookie Gyrl. See her photo below, with a reward of

$2,000.00. Well that was the worst thing I could have ever done. Now I get folks knocking on my door with any ole cat that has an iota of a resemblance. They even tried dying a cat's hair to make it look like Pookie. Heck, people were knocking on my door at all hours of the day and night. Man I couldn't sleep a wink! So then to put a stop to this fiasco, I posted another sign saying Pookie was found. So please don't come to my house. Reward was paid out, and besides I won't be home. Second mistake, now they're trying to burglarize my home. Now I got to get me a ferocious dog that will deter any more robbery attempts. I guess those thieves thought if I could pay out a handsome reward then I must be fully loaded. Fully loaded alright! With a shotgun in case you have other ideas. So don't test me or make my day, ciao . . .

That's the Reward sign of Pookie Gyrl I put up all around the neighborhood asking for her return, big mistake!!!

LOST CAT!!!
$2,000.00 REWARD!!!
INQUIRE WITHIN OR CONTACT THE AUTHORITIES

I got some good news that has me spinning like a top. I'm now the proud owner of a new business. It's called 'Mooner For Hire.' I moon folks for money. I'm here to report that it's a money maker. All I have to do is drop my pants, and my money maker comes out, hahaha, don't ask. So call me when you want me to embarrass someone. It can be your ex-husband, ex-wife, your boss, your lawyer, your teacher, your mayor, your preacher, your mailman, your milkman, your mother, father, or a sibling. Heck, it don't matter who! Just show me the money, hahaha!!!

Folks, I got a story to tell you. You can add 'Wheeler/Dealer' to my long list of jobs to my distinguished resume. What's a Wheeler/Dealer? Glad you asked! I wheel and deal. Let's say you want something. Well that's where I come in. I can get you that something. You want to meet a celebrity? No problem! Why last night I hooked up this hot babe with Boy George, don't ask. Last week this girl wanted Chuck Berry's autograph. So I contacted a friend who knew a friend who had a friend who personally knew Chucky. But I did one better. I got Chucky to give up his cowboy boots, and he signed them too! He wrote, "To my ding a ling friend, yours truly Chuck Berry." Hey, you want to meet Clint Eastwood's barber? For the right price I can get you Clint's lock of hair, or Tina Turner's old dancing nylon stockings. I got it all and then some!!!

Folks, I got a story to tell you, like Bette Davis, I'm a spy. I can tell you stories that will curl your toes, and have the hair on your neck standing at attention. I can't reveal the places I've been to but let's just say Scotland Yard, Interpol, the CIA, the FBI, and even that Pink Panther all want me. No, not like they are after me. They want me to work for them. That's how good I am. But please don't tell anybody because I also got a lot of enemies. They might try to do me harm. Yep, even kill me! So mums the word. I'm really a 'Secret Agent Man.' I told Johnny Rivers all about me. He wrote a song about my adventures. Double O Seven, has nothing over on me. Well, I got to go! Batman is calling me. He and I are likethis hahaha.

By the way, he introduced me to Cat Lady, umm, umm, umm, say no more!!!!!
(Play Johnny Rivers' song "Secret Agent Man")

I'm going to tell you something I've never told anybody before. I'm tore up from the floor up. You all heard of Evel Knievel. Yep—that motorcycle death defying stunt crazy man. Well like him, I'm like a bucket of bolts. I have so many nuts and bolts in my body. I always fail the metal detector test whenever I fly. The TAS folks at the airports give me the once over, and they really earn their pay. But why did they make me bend over? That was just too much. It violated my privacy. I got pins in my shoulders, knees, wrists, and fingers. But not up my butt. So yes, I am put together, and held together by tons of screws, nuts and bolts. They ought to call me the tin man, see you!!!

Folks, my cowboy days have come to an end. It ended when that mechanical bull threw me off. I was out cold for two hours. So I'm taking up space travel. Yep, I want to go where nobody's gone before, explore the universe, and if I'm lucky meet aliens. The female type is really what I seek. I heard they're out of this world. Uncle Sam is looking for some good men and women to take a journey to the unknown. So I'm going back to the basics. Getting my body in tip top shape because I already have an excellent mind. But the body needs a little tweaking. I should be ready in no time. Hey, my first mission is to the moon and back. If any of you girls are looking for a good time, I'm your man! Heaven will be our final destination, ooooooo weeeeeee!
(Play Jonathan King song "Every One's Gone To The Moon")

Folks, I got a story to tell you. In my resume, I stated I was a 'Graveyard Digger.' Well that was half the truth. I neglected to tell you, it's part of an illegal operation, my 'Hit Man' business. When I did a hit (killed somebody), I would bury two or three bodies in the same pit. You know an unmarked hole in the ground or in a wall. Then I would do the humane thing like plant some flowers (roses, irises, or tulips) on top. In some situations, I applied Plaster of Paris to close the hole in the wall, and hide the smell. Which by the way, I could get cheap at that home improvement store where I work part-time. Anyway, that's what I do. I kill people for a price. So if you want me to kill someone, or a group, I'm your man! What do you say? Do you want somebody dead? Then call me, and let's do business, hahaha.

Folks, whenever I want to get the latest news and gossip in town, I run over to my barber shop because those guys know everything and anything. Heck, they even know how to balance the U.S. National budget. President Obama should come over if he knows what's good for him. Joseppi, Rolando, and Cisco could easily become the next top-rated anchormen in America. Well at least in my neighborhood! Hey, do you want to know who's fooling around, begetting who, where and when? Go to the barber shop. They know everybody's business. They even told me that my upstairs neighbor Yolanda Benderupper strips for tips at that new bar 'Whiskey A-Go-Go'. Well, that's none of my business! But I do have an urge for a cold one. I might drop on over later. No, not what you're thinking! Just to wet my whistle. See you and be good or be good at it, ciao!!!

Folks, do you recall your younger days? No, further than that, your elementary school days? Well, I can! Let me tell you about one of my sisters who I consider to be, both a moron and a scholar. Why a moron? Well, when she was in the first grade, she would never respond to the teacher, who called out her name, Luisa. She knew herself to be Nilsa, not Luisa. And when nobody in the class would respond, all the kids would be turning their heads looking for that Luisa girl, including Luisa. They must have thought that's one dumb kid. But let me tell you how smart she really was. See, she was very shy to raise her hand to ask the teacher if she could go to the bathroom. No siree Bob! So, she would just pee right there in that seat. She would move to another chair when she felt sticky, wet, or embarrassed. Now, tell me she wasn't smart. Brighter than a light bulb, that's her alrighty! Well, now you know why she was both a dumbbell and an Einstein. See, you some other time with more of my family history secrets, ciao!!!

Folks, is it just me or do you know somebody who loves to gossip. I mean it can be your neighbor, your husband, your sister, or even your mother. Let me tell you what happened to me a few years back. I was scheduled for a hernia operation. During this time, one of my sisters was spreading gossip about me to the family. So I decided to confirm my suspicions. I would tell her I was also having extras being done. I figured since I'm on the table, the doctor could spin me around, and give me a butt job. You know, like a boob job except they stick those bags in my butt cheeks, left and right. Then after that they can spin me around again, and give me a penis enlargement. Well in reality, I was only having a hernia operation. A few days later, I called my other sisters, and sure enough they knew the whole nine yards. That's when I busted out laughing, and told them the truth. I just wanted to confirm my suspicions, and make a fool out of my sister. It proved she was the one spreading my business all over town. Thanks for hearing me out. Have a good day! Watch your backs, ciao . . .

Folks, I don't recall if I ever told you I met Ray Charles? Yep, twenty years ago and we got to become drinking buddies. He loved wine, especially Thunderbird, oooooooooooo weeeeeeeeeeee. Why I say loved? Because he's no longer with us. Well, back to my story. I was involved in an auto accident, and it left me with back spasms. They rushed me to the hospital a block away. There Ray Charles, my idol, was as clear as day, lying in a bed next to me, in the emergency room. His chauffeur hit a tree. Ray's left leg was badly damaged. I heard the doctor tell him they would have to amputate it. Oh, I was so devastated that I cried. But then I heard the doctor say, "But you got the right one baby, uh huh!" Boy was that a relief! It was good to know, he'll be on a good foot!!!

I got to tell you a story. Just like those mama jokes, when guys get together they love to tear people apart. There's always a ringleader or two. Then you need an audience. So on this one particular day, during my lunch break, they were picking on this new Russian employee, from the hills of Siberia or Mongolia whose English was very limited. After a fifteen minute barrage of constant verbal abuse and insults the ringleader said, "What do you got to say?" Mind you this was his one and only opportunity to say something in his defense. So he looked at him straight in the eyes and said, "Dickhead!" We all busted out laughing. He made his point clear with just one word or is it two, no, one, hahaha. Have a nice day . . .

Folks, you remember my friend Mickey? Yeah, my partner in crime, who between the two of us gave Mikey Lugo that botched haircut. Well, Mickey was known as a ringleader, the lowest and meanest of them all. He'd get an audience together and they would poke fun at anyone around. Let him tell you this story:

Hey, don't believe everything Jimmy says. He's just jealous because I always get the girls. Well enough about him. At a former job, I worked for a trucking outfit where I prepped all the trucks for the next day's deliveries. There was a guy that worked with me named Chavos. His real name was Perez. So I would say, "Chavos why the heck are you working here? You are too good for us! You're an educated man of the world. And besides, you'll only get your hands dirty. You should be a lawyer, a doctor, anything but a warehouse worker." And the boys would be laughing. Perez knew we were making him the butt of our jokes. Sometimes I would belittle him too much, that he would later ask me, "Did I kill your brother?" And then I would just smile, embrace him and apologize for my stupid behavior. Like always he would forgive me, and hope this would be the last of me ridiculing him. Nope! The next day it would start all over again. Thanks! Btw Jimmy is lucky I don't reveal some of the things I've done to him! Fuhgettaboudit! Hey, those are my words, not his! Glad to have met you all, bye bye!!!

Folks, I'm going to tell you what got me through in corporate America, and in life. When you are looking for a job, and I don't care what it is, a proctologist, a plumber, a stockbroker, a chief bottle washer, whatever, when you go to that interview, all I ask is that you come fully prepared. Put on your best suit! By all means shit, shower, shave, and be there on time. Combing your hair, shining your shoes, and ironing your clothes is a must. Last but not least, have a pencil in your pocket. You see the latter was what did it for me. I was surrounded by folks with PHD's and degrees up the yang, yang! But what they all lacked was a writing utensil. Of the three dozen applicants there looking to get that janitor job, I was the only qualified candidate. It was all on account that I had a pocket full of pencils. Now I sit in an office at the corner of the building. I have a private secretary, too. And yes, it also pays to know someone on the top. My granddaddy founded the place. It's called 'Hurts Rent a Plane.' My name is Dick Hurts. You might be familiar with an incident when I was locked up for dabbling. Yep, when I went to get me a screw. Well that's a long story but I did have to change my name to Jimmy. Ciao and how . . .

Folks, I got a secret to tell you. In my profile, I neglected to say I'm also a 'Con Man.' To paraphrase my good friend Tina Turner, "Simply the best, better than all the rest!" Let me school you some! Anyone interested in owning a piece of the Brooklyn Bridge or of the London Bridge? Well I'm the man who can make that happen. I know what you're thinking—No way Jose! Heck, I can get anything you want. You want a moon rock or water from the moon? Then consider it done. When do you want it? I'll have it in two days, so put your order in soon, before it's gone, ciao!!!

This week when you buy a rock from the moon (they make excellent nut crackers), you get an eight ounce cup of water also from the moon for free. Hurry while supplies last!

I also got some nuts and bolts from the Brooklyn Bridge. So how many do you want? There's a limit of 100 dozen per household. Let's see, $396.89 a dozen, times 100. Well you do the math! Hurry, before the supplies run out. Send me the money, cash on delivery. Be the first on your block to own a piece of the rock, well not rock, a bucket of bolts is more like it.

Folks, I got a confession to reveal. I was one mad dude. So mad I spent a few years in lockup at the state asylum. But I'm ok now. Trust me, I won't burn down your house nor steal your copper plumbing pipes. And here's some more good news, I beat out 200 other nut jobs in the basket weaving competition held at Bellevue Hospital. And you're looking at the thumb twiddling champion, three years running. I'm so good, I can even twiddle my thumbs upside down, and even in my sleep. If that's not enough, I can catch my thumb at will. So you can say, I'm gifted. I always knew I was talented and a rare breed. Ciao, it's time for my electric shock treatment, and there's no need to strap me up. Just put me on that gurney, and shock it to me, ooooooooooo weeeeeeeeeee!!!

Hey folks, especially anyone who is of Irish or Scottish descent, I got a question for you. Those bagpipers that you see marching in those parades, weddings, or funerals. I'm sure you know what I'm leading up to. Is it true they wear nothing underneath? Why I ask? It's because I was planning on wearing an outfit like that on Halloween. I needed to know the proper attire. An Irish friend of mine tells me they don't wear a thing underneath! So what do you think? Do they, or don't they? Just want to know for the record. Those Irish people always seem to have a different story depending on who you ask. Let me know, ok! Send it right here to Radio City Music Hall c/o my good friend Mel B. She's off the hook and spot on hot ooooooooooo ooooooooooo ooooooooooo, ciao!!!

Folks, let me ask you a question. Is it just me and Eric Clapton who believe that when you're doing well, you know, got a lot of spending loot from an inheritance, from winning at the ponies, hitting the lotto that everybody seems to know your name? They even want to be your long-lost friend, your lover, and they can't compliment you enough. They even drop by your house day and night, 24/7, to break bread and drink whatever you've got to drink. But the minute your chips are down, the booze runs dry, nobody but nobody, wants to know you. All of a sudden, you're like the plague. Well, when I do get back on my feet again, who knows win the America's got Talent title, I'll be the king of the hill. But in the meantime I'm going to do what that Sinatra fella did. Roll myself up in a ball and fly. Might even book a ticket, and split this here town for good. Get me some real down-to-earth friends. Know any? Send them my way! Those with some spending loot, and looking for a real man. Yep me! Thanks and don't call me, I'll call you!
(Play Frank Sinatra song "That's Life")

I was thinking about when I depart this here good earth, how do I want to go out? In a casket or in an urn? And then it hit me! In a can of chock full of nuts. You know that heavenly coffee tin. I hear it's the best money can buy. Yep, save my family the added expense of an expensive box. That I can't take with me no how. So that's my last request. Maybe my heirs will auction it off to the highest bidder. PT Barnum once said, "There's a sucker born every minute!" I got a feeling they'll be one or two takers, hahaha, bye bye!!!

In the winter months the blood banks are always looking for some good men and women. They're on the prowl for some fresh blood. They try to lure you in with a promise of a free t-shirt or a button. But every time I give some, I have to be blindfolded. You see, I can't stand the sight of blood especially mine. I have this fear I'm going to bleed out. But it's for a good cause. Another good cause is donating your body parts so others may live. So carry your drivers ID and sign that donor card section that allows them to harvest your organs for transplants. Thanks . . .

By the way, I'm not just an advocate and a donor. I'm also a recipient of an arm transplant. But you already heard that story before, and you can believe it or not!!!

Guys, I need to know have any of you ever received a "Dear John Letter?" That's a letter a woman who has no 'cojones' sends to a man that their relationship is over, finished, finito! I can't make it any clearer than that. Well, if you were that John fella, know it could end your world. The TV series is based on a group of misfits who meet to discuss their failures in life, and their hopes of putting their lives back in some kind of order. I was once a member of such a group. We conspired on how to get even with our spouses. We even thought of burning their houses down to the ground. But that's for another time, and another story. We did a lot of things together like join nudist clubs, party till we were drunk, and got over on our dating mates, hahaha! Can't say no more because I was one little devil. Ok, ok one mean, cold, callous, conniving devil! Ciao and how . . .

Hey, now you can add 'Chef' to my already highly decorated resume. It started two months ago, when I was on 'You Tube' trying to pick up some pointers in the art of cooking. You see, I like to experiment. I came up with some exotic food recipes of my own inventions. Here check them out: Wild Rooster Mango, Upside Down Turtle Legs Casserole, Peacock A La King, and Pigeon on a Canopy. Oh, I can go on and on! But I must be honest, it really started twelve years ago when I did my layover at the Rahway State Prison for that botched-up bank heist. Yes, I got caught and sentenced to eleven years (where as my sidekick only got sixty days). Why's that? Because they thought she was too old to go to the pokey. Too old my foot! She's the one who raised me. She should have done those eleven years, not I. Who was she? She was my grandmother Ida who fell asleep at the wheel of our getaway car. Anyway, I took up cooking in prison. In no time, I became head chef after my two superiors mysteriously came down with ptomaine poisoning. They never caught the culprit responsible for their demise. But I rather we change the subject. Hey, I will be more than honored if any of you folks, especially you sexy gals in the audience, would be so kind as to send me some of your recipes. It would be preferred that we get together, and exchange recipes over some stiff drinks.

Btw, you want that ptomaine poison recipe? Send me a self-addressed, stamped envelope where you could be located, and who it is you want out of your misery? Thanks again! Don't feel bad! You too can be anything you want. You just have to have 'cojones' and a whole bunch of desires. Got to go! I'm going to make pastrami on a bed of snake casserole using a whole wheat bun, umm umm umm. Yeah, I am starting to eat healthy in case I do hook up with some babes!!!

Folks, I got some good news but you better hold on tight because what I got to say will blow you, and me away. I was talking to my fortune teller last night. That gypsy said, her crystal ball told her, I was going to meet a woman, possibly two, but one was freaky. How freaky? One had thirteen toes, that's how freaky! Well, now a days, freaky is in, and those are the kind of ladies I like, don't ask. I'm going to party like there's no tomorrow. If you don't hear from me any time soon, then know I'm in good hands. How's that? Two of them, one of me, and you go figure. Do I need to draw you a picture? Didn't think so! Bye, bye, so long, farewell! I'm a man on a mission, ménage a three . . .

Folks, please raise your hand if you are a lawyer or related to one. Good, please keep that in mind for the record. Well for the rest of you, the non-lawyers, did you know that the lowest form of slime on the face of the earth are lawyers? They will take it all. Here you thought they were out to protect you. Well, I got news for you—all they got on their minds is where to get that next dollar. You see them chasing ambulances, day in and day out, 24/7, and do you know why? Because that's money in their pockets. They can smell it a mile away. They have one rule—just follow the money. Well, I'm going to be a lawyer someday. I watch all them lawyer shows. I've seen so many divorce court episodes that I can be a divorce court lawyer in no time. It don't matter which side I'm on, just as long as I get my fair share. I know how to be slick as some of those slicksters. They would have to get up before the rooster, in order to pull a Willie over my eyes. I have eyes like an eagle, and sharp to the kill. That'll be me alrighty, Jimmy ESP, LLC. & CO.

Folks, I got a tip I want to share with you that got me through life and helped me be the man I am today. When you go on a job interview there are three things you should have on your person. One, clean shoes, two, a bow tie, and last but not least, three, a pencil, and the more the better. You see I've gone to interviews, and all around me were some of the smartest people on the face of the earth. But they all lacked one of these three things that I mentioned above. Three things that would seal the job for them. These candidates had diplomas up the yang yang. Some even spoke two or three languages fluently, which in today's world is a must. Me, I hate to brag but I speak half a dozen languages. I speaka Spanish, Italiano, gutter talk, freaking Scottish or Irish, same shit, and parley vous Frenchy. So you know, I know how to get over. The reason I always beat out those candidates is because I was the most equipped candidate. I always responded with "Yes Sir!", or "No Mam!" So they could see, I had proper etiquette. What am I doing today? I give motivational seminars in prisons. Many of those folks come to my courses because they want to be successful like me. I am known as—Mr. Big Stuff! Well, hope to see you, and please, please if nothing else bring a pencil wherever you go . . . (Play Jean Knight song "Mr. Big Stuff")

When I hook up with a woman the first thing I look for is if she's got a diary. You see after dating her for a day or two, I figure if I'm the man in her life, I will see that in her writings. Last week, my current squeeze allowed me to move in. She was impressed with me, the kid! I guess my nightcap rendezvous sealed the deal. So as she stepped outside to do some errands, it gave me some time to search for a diary. Right there, in the top draw of her/our bedroom dresser, there was, a diary. So I opened it up, and sure as I'm telling you this story, she had written some very intimate romantic details of our relationship. I can't say what because what two consenting adults do in the bedroom, up against the walls, in the halls, on the floors, and on the roof is only for our ears and eyes. Let's just say I am the most with my manhandling. Well, got to go! We got plans for a hot bubble bath, capped with a whole body massage. Just another chapter for her to write in that diary, oooooooooooo weeeeeeeeeee!

Folks, I got some news to tell you. I'm going to start my own hair cutting business. No, I don't have a license, nor do I need one. I'm experienced and that's all that matters. I'll put a bowl over your freaking head and clip away. What gave me the idea was when I was going through some old photos, and there we were, Mickey, Mikey and me. What's that got to do with my hair cutting business? Back in the day, when we were eleven or twelve, Mickey and I gave Mikey our first professional haircut. Yep, on Mikey's noggin. One look at Mikey and one would say we butchered him good and tight. But when you consider it was our first, it was a masterpiece in our eyes. Mikey and his father didn't think so. But 'C'est la vie' is all I got to say! Besides, we saved Mikey's father the two dollars it would cost to cut Mikey's hair. Oh yeah, we avoided walking past Mikey's building in fear we might bump into his father. He was a tough cookie. That was before anybody heard of Mike Tyson. We heard stories of Mr. Lugo, and how he would use

Mikey and his siblings like a punching bag. So we didn't take any chances. Well back to me—I can give you any hairstyle you want! There's the Mohawk look, the Kojak look, a Caesar, a high and tight, and a # one, or a # two. Heck, I can even put your initials on the back of your head, or if you prefer, your sweetheart's initials. So if you're in town, look me up, at Jimmy's Barber Shop on Steinway St. and 30th Avenue. It's where your dollar goes a long way! And for you ladies, you're in luck too! I can give you a Brazilian waxing. You'll be looking sharp, once I get through with you. There's no need to tip me! It's my pleasure. I might be tipping you! Don't ask, hahaha, bye, bye, so long, farewell . . .

For those of you who aren't aware, I'm a 'Junk Collector.' I go to flea markets every chance I get looking for some genuine artifacts that I can resell at a higher price and make a quick buck. Sometimes I come across a rare music album or a genie lamp. Well, last Friday I was ready to leave when I came across this naked mannequin. It reminded me of the time when I was a kid of thirteen and I had an inflatable doll. I rather not talk about this but I can say my friends loved it. They would come over, pretend it was a real girl, dance with it, hold it, and do all sorts of things. They would practice their dance moves in case they had the nerve to go to the Friday and Saturday Night Sock Hops. There they could ask one of the girls to dance. My best friend who will remain anonymous, borrowed it one night and when he brought it back, a month later, it had patches all over it. When I asked him why the holes? He said, his belt buckle popped it every time he took it for a spin. I think Mickey took it for more than a whirl like maybe slowed danced with it or some shit. What became of that doll? My mother caught one of the Shane brothers, Michael or Robert, kissing it in the lips and squeezing it to death. She put a match to it. Hey, let's not mention this ever again! People may get the wrong ideas. I was thinking I could dress up that mannequin for the holidays, like a snow woman, the Easter Bunny, or maybe just use it for target practice. I got me a pistol that I can use on it. You know what they say, practice makes perfect. I'm perfect but that's another story for another day!

Folks, I got a question to ask you. What do you do when you get unexpected visitors or visitors who don't know when it's time to go home? Oh, this is one dilemma I can't resolve on my own. So if you know how I should handle this situation, please help me out! My daughter thinks I should say, "Here's your hat! What's your hurry?" Maybe I'll try that approach next time that somebody comes over, and see if that works. Ok, ok it's my mother-in-law. She comes over at all hours of the day, wants to eat me out of house and home. She's one ugly good for nothing, bloodsucking creature from down under. I don't mean Australia, deeper than that, ciao!!!

For you folks new to my channel, I'm a 'Pretender'! I like to pretend where I work in the plumbing aisles. What's a pretender? Thought you'd never ask! When I want to impress an old acquaintance or a hot chick, I get into my pretender persona. I simply put on my clip-on bow tie. I yell out an order to one of my co-workers that the next time they come in late I'm going to have to let them go. I will pretend I'm on my IPhone giving orders to my chauffer, to have my Rolls Royce ready in half an hour. Hahaha, I know, that's crazy! My co-workers scratch their heads, think to themselves that I'm a freaking maniac! Well, it is things like that which have promoted me to other positions within the store, especially in the plumbing department. I no longer have to push a broom or work the graveyard shift because I'm also an 'Ass Kisser.' Whenever I see the boss coming, I say things like, you look good today! I see you lost some weight!, and I just love your shirt! Well, he hasn't lost weight. In fact, he has put on a few pounds. He wears the same old shirt every day. But the compliments get me a smile and a big ole thank you. Get this, he invited me to his house for the holidays. I told him I couldn't make it because I was dining with the Marquis of England, and the next day going on a fox hunt with Sir William of Scotland. Well, now you know how I suck up to people and why I'm the best at what I do. Ciao, the Queen is calling me. I wonder what she wants from me now, byeeeee . . .

Guys always ask me why am I so successful with the ladies? What is it that I do? Well, I hate giving away my trade secrets but I do know the art of seduction. First, you got to set the trap. Well, not really a trap, just get the right atmosphere in motion to make that lady putty in your arms. A romantic dinner for two with scented candles is a must! Have a good bottle of booze to get her at ease to open up. Then you put on some soft romantic music like a little Freddie Jackson, some Al Green, Michael Bolton, The Delfonics, Smokey, Teddy, and last but not least, Barry White. By this time, she should be ripe for the taking. Get her on the dance floor, lay down some of your best sweet talking lingo, and whisper a few sweet nothings in her ears. This will drive her up the wall, and bingo she's all yours! You top it off with a choice of—a hot steamy bubble bath or a massage to kill for, with some ying yang massage oil. Be the gentleman that you are! Let her choose her poison. She'll respect you for that. It always works for me.

By the way, don't forget to put up that 'Do Not Disturb, Gone Fishing!' sign, hahaha!!!

Hey, in case you haven't figured it out by now, I was a misfit most my adolescent years. By the time I started shaving, I had a record as long as my arm. Yep, I got into all kinds of trouble, like the time I was sent to reformatory school for beating up my third grade teacher, Ms. Ratched. Well, she didn't have to bite me, kick me, or pull my hair. I just retaliated but with a lot of force and gusto. Also, whenever I had a sleepover at my house, I would invite two or three friends on the weekend. What we did to one of the kids is a crying shame. We would go off to sleep at midnight, after looking at a bunch of girlie magazines. I'd wake up one or two of the guys, and we would do some crazy shit. Paint the other guy's toe nails, neon green or hot pink, while he was asleep. Then with my sister's makeup kit, we'd paint his eyebrows twice the size, and slap on some bright red lipstick. Presto! He'd be looking like a hot child from the city. The next morning we would get up early laughing because he didn't know what we did to him during the night. Upon looking into the mirror, he almost had a heart attack. Quickly, he jumped into the tub, took a long hot shower and was able to remove most of the makeup. Except he looked like he had two black eyes. His toe nails were a different story. Anything he did, could not remove that paint. So I told him, when he got home, to rub some turpentine over his nails. That should do the trick! He would never do another sleepover ever again. We called him Roxanne. Hey, here's the clincher! We took some glossy photos of him. Every now and then we blackmail him for money. I know I was wicked but then that's why I always ended up in reformatory school or in jail. Hey, don't do any sleepovers at my house. You'll never live it down. Btw, hot pink toe nails is in! Try it, you might like it!!!

Folks, have you've heard the expression—'My boat has come in!' Well, it's coming to me in a big way. Let me start from the beginning. I'm seeing this big name celebrity who currently has a show of her own. For the record, her name will remain anonymous. Who is she? Hey, didn't I explain myself clearly? A gentleman never tells. We met when I was an audience member on her show. I was all dressed up with nowhere to go. She spotted me in the crowd. I was wearing my new spandex, hot pink outfit and matching, pink go-go boots. That was all she had to see. She invited me over to her house for a nightcap. I showed her my all. She showed me her all. Before you knew it, we made love the whole night through. Now get this, she's going to have my baby, and that's why I say, "My boat has come in!" I won't have to work ever again except to pamper that woman and my child to be. Hey, don't tell anybody because it will get into the tabloids. Then every paparazzi will be following me all over town. Well, I hope you're all excited for me. Maybe I'll invite you to my wedding. When's that? When I hook it up. She's got a way about her. So when I wrap her around my fingers some more, then maybe I will pop the question. She's going to love the kid. I will take her to heaven and the moon! Heck, anywhere she wants to go! She's got limos, boats, planes, and now me. Hey, her boat's come in too, hahaha!!!

I've told you many things about me but not everything. So I'm going to tell you something I've never told anybody. I'm an eccentric S.O.B. How's that? Good question?

When I walk outside, I don't step on cracks. I run indoors when I see or hear a bus or a truck coming. I'm afraid of the noise and the pollution they emit. When a plane or a helicopter passes overhead, I also run inside. I think they're going to crash down on me. And if that's not enough, I'm even afraid of my own shadow. I think it's following me and out to choke me. My therapist says I'm nuts. I guess she's right. She's the one with all the plaques and awards all over her walls. Plus, it takes one to know one. A person can't be too careful nowadays. Hey, that's not all! I never take an elevator, especially with other people inside of it. They give me the jitters like if they are going to stab me. If I hear a fire truck or a police car with its sirens on, I'm crouching underneath the nearest car. That too scares the hell out of me. Oh boy, here comes an ambulance, and you know what that means. Hey, didn't you hear the words that were coming out of my mouth? Get on the ball you freaking morons . . .

Here's another story I've never told anybody before. I've been with my girl now for over three years, two months, and three days. But who's counting? Well she's everything a man could possibly want: gorgeous, witty, caring, and sweeter than a honey bee. But she's got one flaw. Now I know you've heard of folks being born with an extra finger or toe. Well, honey bunch got thirteen toes. She wears clodhoppers to hide it from the public. But here's the best part. When we get to making love, she wraps her feet around me and that girl can go! Need I explain or draw you a picture. That woman makes love to die for! Yep, it's the extra toes that give her that added giddy up! I'm really blessed. Hey, maybe what you need is a woman like that. She'll bring you plenty of joy, and drive you silly. Got to go, it's time I paint her toe nails, and then paint the town red ooooooooooooo weeeeeeeeeeeee!!!

I was talking to my therapist, and that woman told me I should reinvent myself. Now that's a problem because when I look around they already have invented everything man can possibly want, ok, ok and women. I mean the wheel has been here since the time of the modern caveman and pockets on t-shirts! God only knows when? So what is it that I can invent? Hey, if you know the answer to that let me know. We'll go 50 50. No, really! You get 50 and I get 50. I'm as honest as the day is long. See you! Going back to bed. Hopefully to dream of something, anything to make me rich!!!

I got it, I got it, when you go to the beach what is it that you see on men? Let me put it another way. Have you noticed how men are getting top heavy? So why not invent a man bra or a one piece suit for men? It will be similar to the suits for women. I mean a bosom on a lady is phenomenal. On a man, it is disgusting! So that will be my contribution to society. It will become, one giant step for man, one giant leap for me, hahaha.

People ask me is there any particular place where to hook up with the opposite sex? Yes, siree Bob, I know such a place! It's anywhere there are people. I like to find my women at a local library, at a fruit stand, in a museum, at a coffee shop, or in a movie theater, especially during those romantic flicks when girls come alone. If you're lucky and play your cards right, you might get to take her home. Me, I shuffle right into an empty chair next to one. Within time, a minute or two later, I offer her some popcorn, and a slug of booze from my gold pocket decanter. If I'm lucky, she gets drunk, horny or both. Presto! She'll be calling me daddy o! And to the nearest park bench we go, hahaha. Also, last but not least, in a bar is another place to hook up. Now in a bar you got to be extra careful because once you start to drink, the dog inside of you comes out. What do I mean? You're getting a buzz, and at this point in time, anything on two legs looks good, even the ugly ones look good for the taking, hahaha. And before you know it, it's a bara bing, bara bang, thank you mame! Well, I got to go wet my whistle. We're due for an encore, ciao . . .

Hey folks, every now and then, when I need some spending loot, I throw a yard sale event. I'll post a, 'Going out of business!' sign. That's when folks by the droves come over expecting to find some good stuff. Remember someone's junk is another one's treasure. I got some old used underwear. Why chuck them, when I can find a sucker to buy them for a nickel each. That's a nickel in my pocket, an old fruit of the loom, one of a kind underwear for some cheap so and so. Yes, one hand washes the other. Well, if you're smart come on over. They say the early worm catches the bird or something like that. But you get my drift. You got to be there to score big at my yard sales. I got an old trench coat I found in Columbo's trash can. Now tell me you wouldn't want to own it. Hey, Columbo had his use for it. Just not useful any more to him but it would surely look good on you. So hurry over. I got many other—one of a kind deals! I got an old Elvis scarf, and one of his shoes. Why one? Because I donated the other one to the 'Smithsonian Institute for the Blind,' hahaha don't ask, byeeeeee.

By the way, can you use Madonna's bra or a Simon Cowell old t-shirt that he wore on 'American Idol?' Well I can get them, but never mind where I get them. Just tell me what you want, when, and the size because I can make it happen! They don't call me the Handy Man for nothing!!!
(Play Jimmy Jones song "The Handy Man")

When I was in mid-school, Charlie Brown was our idol and everybody wanted to be just like him. He was the delinquents' greatest hero. Why? That boy singlehandedly drove the teachers and principals insane with his antics. He would instigate spitball fights the

minute the teachers turned away. When he spoke it was more like—"What the heck did he just say?" He talked with his daddy-o lingo that we never fully understood. I can recall whenever a teacher tried to lecture him for his crazy antics, that his replies always drove them mad. All he would say was, "huh." Oh, they wanted to kill him right there and then. But I guess there were too many witnesses. I mean the boy could do no wrong. He would do graffiti on the walls, like "Eat at Joe's, or at your mama's." Or when he thought the building was way too hot, he'd pull the fire alarm so all the kids could catch a breather when they had to evacuate the building. When he went to gym, he would always find an excuse not to build up a sweat. He said things like, he banged his toe in the auditorium or his house burned down last night. Therefore, he didn't get enough sleep and to wake him when it's time to go home. I mean that boy was crazy like a fox and smarter than a third grader. Oh, what a clown that Charlie Brown!!!
(Play The Coasters song "Charlie Brown")

For those who don't know, I am the reincarnation of James Dean. Who is James Dean? The baddest movie star that ever lived. Why he could make the womenfolk drool, and put the fear in men. It was he who started me on my career of terror. And that was when I was only eight years old, in the first grade. I was so bad, my teacher would put me in front of the class, standing, facing the corner of the room. Well, that didn't stop me! It just got me started. I would do crazy things. You don't want to know! Ok, ok, I would scratch my butt, cut wind, and I mean good and loud. I would say pardon me, and the class would start laughing, hysterically. The teacher couldn't do a thing because who do you know that doesn't fart? We're all humans and shit does happen. But the truth is, I can fart at command. I guess I have a talent for that too. You don't believe me, here let Nicky boy pull my thumb and see what happens, hahaha. Another thing I would do when the teacher had to leave the room for any type of emergency is that I would gather up all the blackboard erasers, and chuck them out the window. The kids knew better then to squeal on me. If they dared, I would beat them silly after school. They would get two black eyes to show for their good deeds. So when the teacher would come back to resume her lessons, everybody was holding their breath, waiting in anticipation, for when she would have to erase the boards. And when that time did arise, the whole class would burst into tears, laughing. She knew right there and then that I was the culprit. Omg, you should have seen her chasing me around that classroom. She would be in tears. I think she would have strangled me if she had caught up to me. Sure enough the next day I was suspended from class until my mother showed up. As a result, I would get the beating of my life. But then that's why I was called a rebel rouser! Badder than ole King Kong! Yesiree Jimmy Dean was I, ciao!!!

Can you keep another secret? I still confide in my fortune teller. Every week I go over to her office to have a consultation. That's what she calls it now. But it's just a small room in her house, a 6 by 6. If you ask me, it looks more like a broom closet. What's a consultation? What the heck do I know? She calls our readings that! I think it makes her feel important, as if she were a doctor or an engineer with a PHD. Last night, I paid her a visit. She told me I was going to hit the mother lode. So I asked her what she meant by that. She gave me that one-eyed evil look. Yeah, she wears a patch on the other eye, and said, "Sucker you're going to be mingling with the rich and famous." Then I smiled and said "ooooooooooooo weeeeeeeeeeeeee." At first I thought, was I going to meet a hot mama! You know, fully loaded. Then I began to read in between the lines. I realized I'm going to be rich and famous. You do know that I wrote two 'YouTube' blockbuster books! What's a blockbuster? That's when you sell a lot of books, a couple of hundred or more and people start calling you sir. Has it happened yet? No, but I know it's going to happen one day soon. Well, I got to go! My agent is calling me. That jerk probably wants some more money. I pay her by the week. She gets plenty of me, don't ask, hahaha, byeeeeeee!!!

Folks, you can add 'Ass Kisser' to my resume. Yep, I polish apples for my boss, and that's not all I do for her. I'm the rat in the vessel at my workplace. I tell her who's not working, who's doing who, who took an extra break, stole a pen, or some paper clips. I'm a one of a kind snitcher. Best of the best, and nothing gets past me. Well, got to go! Here comes a shady co-worker. I'm going to keep an eye on her, ciao!!!

My therapist thinks because I love making pottery I got a feminine side about me. Well she doesn't know the whole story. I invite girls over so I can teach them how to make pottery. But the real reason is so I can seduce them. See as I sit behind them, I get to feel them, and that's my way of teasing them. That leads to a little wrestling, a skip and a hop, to my 'man cave bed.' I got the idea from watching the movie 'Ghost'. Starring Patrick Swayze, Demi Moore, and Whoopi Goldberg. I got a basement full of pottery. One day I'm going to throw a going out of business pottery sale. Do you need any ash trays or cups? I got them! You want to learn how to make pottery? I'm your man! Just book an appointment. Yeah, I got lots of women who want me. I mean who wants me to teach them the how to of pottery? You will just love me! Ciao and let's do lunch for starters . . .

When I was a kid I would watch 'The Little Rascals' every morning before going off to school. Alfalfa, Buckwheat, Spanky (just to name a few) were some of the main characters. Oh yeah, let's not forget Darla too. It was about a bunch of kids just like all kids growing up and facing the world. Probably no different than when you or I were kids. Well, I always got to school late as a result. The teacher would say "What is it this time Jimmy?" and I would always find an excuse. Like, "My mother lost my homework but lucky for me I found it in her cookie jar!" See I was a con man/kid back then too. Well, it was one particular episode that caused me to run away from home, and join the circus. When I first joined up, they had me cleaning up after the elephants, then the tigers, and gorillas. But then my break came through when the headliner of The Flying Trapeze came down with an unexpected bout of scurvy. I wonder what could have brought that upon him, hahaha. Yep, it was me! I added some elephant, you know what, into his soup. And he got sick. The poor boy never knew what hit him, hahaha. So I volunteered to go up. And that was the start of my new profession. The greatest trapeze artist of all time. Maybe you heard of me, Don Jimmy & his Flying Deuces, ciao . . .

I got a story to tell you. Have you ever heard of the 'Dodo Bird?' It was thought to have disappeared from the face of the earth, back in the sixteen hundreds. It was put on the extinct list. Well, I got some good news and some bad news to report. The good news is that it's no longer extinct. Now for the bad news, there's a bunch of them nesting at my job sight and they haven't changed a bit. They are lazy and dumb as ever. I'm going to inform 'Wild Kingdom', 'National Geographic Society' and Simon Cowell to put them back on the still active list. Going to send them the proof. It won't look pretty! They are one ugly bunch. That's how I see those Dodo Birds.

Did I tell you I was once a hot shot on Wall Street? What happened? I lost it all in the market back in 2008. My stockbroker tricked me into buying a piece of the rock. Yeah, I bought everything he told me. Now I'm flat broke, and he's a fat cat mingling with the upper class at some brothel in Mexico. Well, enough of that! I know better this time. I'll spread it out, keep some in my pillow, in my mattress, in the oven, bury some in the back yard, up on the roof, in my basement, and in a safe behind that picture of Pamela Anderson. My agent says I should buy a Picasso! Is he crazy? That would take all his money and mine put together, just for one piece of art. No way! I want something I can feel. Well, you won't have to worry because that's just the beginning. I'll buy some hot commodities like: gold, silver, and copper, a herd of cows, bulls, a bushel of chickens, some oil wells, and futures of OJ, no not him, orange juice, and some underground gas. I'll be rich! I can't get discouraged because sometimes it has to go down but then it has to go back up. It's like a seesaw. Call me if you want in. I'll make you a millionaire just yet, ciao . . .

Whenever I'm lost for words, I ask myself what would Shirley Temple say or do. Then I get inspired and write a revelation of my past experiences. So today I'm going to tell you the time I found a frog, not just any ordinary frog. This frog could jump like no other I have ever seen. Let me start from the beginning. I was driving down the road

minding my own business when I see this frog. I immediately stopped the car. After thirty minutes, I finally capture it, and put it into a duffle bag to take home. Then it hit me, I could make a killing if I enter it into the frog jumping contest at the state fairs. When I got home, I realized I had no place to put it. So I filled up my Jacuzzi and threw the frog into the water. By this time, I was full of mud. So I jumped into the shower to rid me of all this mud that I had accumulated chasing the frog. Unbeknownst to me, my girlfriend Sandra was bringing over four of her co-workers. Angela, Pamela, Rita, and Judy came to soak in the Jacuzzi. So they disrobed down to their birthday suits, and hopped into the Jacuzzi. After about five to ten minutes, they started to feel something crawling onto their feet. So they each popped their heads into the water. And before you can whistle Mambo # 5, they jumped out of the water screaming. So I run out of my tub naked like a jay bird to see what was going on. Lo and behold, there they were—five naked women screaming their lungs out! Before they could say a word, I took my camera and took some photos. I explained that it was an authentic prize, winning, jumping jack frog that I was planning to enter in the State Fairs starting in Minot, ND next July. They sort of settled down a bit but had to cover up so I wouldn't see any more of their naked torsos or take any more photos. We later made a deal. I would give them the photos, if they would show me what they had, with no questions asked. Tonight it's Judy's turn, ooooooooooo oooooooooooo ooooooooooo, say no more, end of story . . .
(Play Leslie Gore song "Judy's Turn To Cry")

A few years back I worked in the Client Changes Department at the ING Minot Service Center in ND. One of the functions we performed on a daily basis was making beneficiary changes on insurance policies. Sometimes a policy owner would request a beneficiary change, deleting a child/sibling. It was requested probably out of a personal dispute between the policy holder and that relative. Then a short time later the owner would request another change, adding that child/sibling back. Sometimes these types of changes would change over and over and over. Ours was not to question why, but to do and die, pardon my pun. Also another change that we always found quite interesting was where one spouse would leave his or her ex-spouse an article of clothing. For example, a leather jacket, or even a bowling ball. Why this request? We felt it was to put an end to a dispute should that beneficiary recipient contest the distribution of the proceeds in court. This request let the courts know the owner was in clear mind when he/she omitted that person from getting any real monetary gain other than that jacket or bowling ball. Well as I always say, something is better than nothing, hahaha.

Folks, I got a story for you that you just aint going to believe. Heck, I don't believe it myself. My friend who will remain anonymous, like hell she will! Her name is Peggy J.

and her husband is called the big game hunter, aka Mr. Bowana J., or the know it all! Well he decides he wants to go lake fishing on New Year's Day. He wants to start the New Year with a bang. So he and his buddy bring along everything needed, including: lots of fishing gear, poles, lures, minnows (you know those little fish used to catch big fish), his favorite pink overall jumpsuit and big heavy duty rubber boots. You just knew he was going to bring along his video camera, and a still camera so he could capture the thrill of victory for posterity. Well, after a few hours (eight to be exact), all they were able to catch was a gallon bucket full of fish barely enough to eat, stuff and mount on the walls. I think it's called taxidermy or some shit. Well, after drinking their four cases of beer, Coronas (he only drinks the best!), which cost five bucks for a twelve pack, they decided it's time to show off their bounty to the boys and wives back home, Peggy included. As they headed out of that frozen tundra they heard the sound of cracking, or was it popping. Well, they heard something and it didn't sound good. That's when his buddy, Lenny, aka Layback Lenny, had the brains to jump out of the vehicle and run for his dear life. He is a smart guy. Now Mr. Bowana J., Peggy's other half, can't say better half because Peggy's got that title. He didn't have the nerve to abandon his prized possession, old Betsy. Yeah, that's what he calls his twenty year old Toyota. He had won it in a card game. Before he could whistle 'Dixie,' his car went down headfirst to the bottom of the lake, with him in it, eight feet down give or take a few inches. Maybe four or five, but who's counting? So he rolled down his window, smart move, and crawls out and floats to the top and hops on an iceberg that just happened to be floating by where he can now get on top and scream his lungs out for help. Now, he can't use his spanking, deluxe brand new phone because it was all wet, and good for nothing. At this point, he is fuming mad, crying his eyes out and wondering how he's going to get back to his lovely bride. She had been watching cartoons and soaps all day long. She's a Looney Tunes freak, and can't stop watching those soap opera programs. Especially, now that Tad is cheating on Snooki from the *Desperate Housewives*, with that one who used to be called Lois Lane from Superman. You know the one. Meanwhile, Bowana J. is mad as hell and wondering how he's going to get back home. So he cons a local farmer with a lure of a deer head, a possum and a squirrel to take him home without his buddy Lenny, who we later found out ran that ten mile stretch all the way home on his own. So Bowana J. arrived home late. Peggy was all cried out, worrying when dinner was going to arrive. Also because her macho man has never been out this late before. So she surmises that he might have kicked the bucket. But, no, that bucket had one gallon worth of fish that he took down with him and most likely got away. Talk about nine lives! They got away with two, but what do I know? Maybe they've been through this before, and are working on lives three or four. Well, the good news is that he made it out alive. The bad news is that he lost everything. As far as the car goes, all they had on it was liability insurance. And now it's sitting at the bottom of the lake, watching the fish that got away swim by. Sad to say, Peggy had to have cereal for dinner, Fruit Loops, and the kid's tuna fish on a roll. I think we have the making for a 'Laurel and Hardy' slapstick movie. Where are they now when we need them? Knowing Peggy's mentality, she is planning a movie and hoping to make a fortune. Maybe with my help it will be a done deal. 50 50, 25 for her and 75 for me. End of story, period.

Do you recall that story I told you earlier today about Peggy's husband? Yeah, Mr. Bowana J. Well, you aint heard the last of it. First of all, let me describe what he looks like. He's a cross between John Wayne, Arnold Schwarzenegger, Rocky Balboa, and Ernest all rolled into one. One mean mother tucker with a vengeance. Well, anyway he took a liking to me because he could see we were both suave and real macho men. Plus, he heard of my reputation as a ladies man. So he invites me over to his log cabin home to show me all his trophies. That boy has all kinds of heads mounted on his walls. Animals include: deer, antelope, possum, rabbits, squirrels, a road hog, and that's just on the first floor. In the basement, he's got a bull's head, a full body spread of an eagle, a hawk, an anaconda, and a queen bee. But on the right wall side, was one big empty hole on the wall. So I said to him, "I see one got away!" He gives me a dirty look. You know the kind that can kill you in a heartbeat. So I said, "Just kidding!" So then he smiles. I asked, "What are you going to put there?" His face changes to a big ole grin. Oh, he has a beautiful grin, even if I say so myself. No, I'm not a fruit cake. I love women. So he replies, "We're going to get it tonight! You should come along." So in a manly voice in front of Peggy I said, "OK!" That night he came to pick me up. Omg! He was dressed to kill. He had guns, knives, and machetes strapped all over his body. He had weapons on his legs and arms. If that was not enough, he wore a camouflage suit, hat included. All I had on was my low cut Hip-hugger Guess Jeans with the stars embroidered every which way, my fruit of the looms, boots, my Levi jacket, and Stetson that I won in a poker game. So after driving six hours up north, we finally arrived to our desired destination. He tells me in a whisper, "We're there." So I said, "Where is there?" So he said, "Devils Ridge!" So he parked his jeep and gathered his other weapons of mass destruction. His William Tell bow and arrow, his 30 yard six, Magnum 44, his Colt 45, and his grenade launcher. Me? All I had was my 22 rifle that comes in a 100% all leather casing. Here I'm thinking he's going for wild turkey or a goose. Had I known he was after bigger fish, I might have stayed home and watched some 'Benny Hill,' 'Mr. Bean' or *Debbie Does Dallas*! So we trek up the mountain. After a half hour, he informs me we're here for mountain lions or bears. That's all I had to hear! So I said, "I don't feel good! I better go back down and rest." He gave me that dirty look again and watched me walk down. The next morning, he showed up all beat down, shirt and pants torn, bleeding like a pig, and dragging what appeared to be a little ole teddy bear. It was no more than fifty pounds. I was so glad he got what he wanted. Now on his wall, is that mean ole little teddy bear! You should have heard him tell the story of how he had to wrestle with it. He was able to put a strangle hold on it for an hour before it succumbed to its death. Don't remind me! Now I know why Peggy fell for this big ole hunk of a man. He would have mounted her head on the wall had she refused his proposal of marriage! Poor Peggy! She must have lived in fear all her life. But then again, she was his biggest catch. She's worth more than all those other heads put together. End of story!!!

Folks, I got an interesting story to tell you. I'm an unofficial member of 'The Polar Bears Club.' On New Year's Day, that group of people go swimming in the Coney Island Beach, and brave the cold waters ranging from 0 to 15 degrees Fahrenheit or colder. Why do we do it? Maybe to prove our manhood/womanhood. But also, it's part of a tradition here in the borough of Brooklyn. Once the home to the famous Brooklyn Dodgers! This coming year 2014, I plan a different approach. I'm going in with my birthday suit. No, you heard it right—buck naked! So if you happen to be in the neighborhood, drop on by to wish me good luck, and for moral support. But beware! There are no cameras allowed, well at least where I'm at. Hey, maybe you shouldn't come! It won't be a pretty sight, especially when I come out of the cold water. You know parts tend to shrivel up. Anyway I'm not going in so don't waste your time coming. I hope not to see you, ciao.

People ask me what I'm really about. Let me begin by telling you my name in Chinese. Hold onto your hats fellas and you ladies better tie a knot on to whatever floats your boat. Here goes: Wun Hung Lo. Well, having said that, I have to admit I know how to treat a lady right. A good woman needs attention, pampering, and good loving. You can call it what you want like sex, to be touched, or manhandled. But it all boils down to feeling wanted and loved. Some call me the handyman. Others call me the masseur because my advice or methods really work. When I'm finished working with my hands, they are fully contented and smiling from ear to ear. No, I can't tell you anymore because each gal is different from the next. My evaluations and hands-on work always do the trick! You know anybody needing my services? Send them over. I'm available 24/7, ciao!!

Folks, I got to make a confession. I'm not all that I pretend to be. I'm just a 'Con Man,' simple and to the point! But I do have the knack of satisfying all the ladies I come in contact with. I can be anything they want me to be: a preacher man, a handy man, your daddy, your lover man. Heck, even your Juicy Fruit Man. See I got what it takes. For instance, if you're down with the blues, I can rid you of them and give you all that you need. You need loving? Well, that's a no brainer! But I can take it a step and you to cloud nine. You don't want to know! Ok, ok, I can put you in a trance and make you a happy camper. You will want to own me once I get through with you, hahaha. By all means call me, free of charge. But yes, a tip is optional. In fact, it's a must! No tip is too small, or too big! Yes, I will barter if you aint got any money. See honey for money will work for me, ciao . . .

(Play Mtumbe song "Juicy Fruit")

Folks, I'm going to share a story with you. One that I've never told anybody. In another life I was a sheik, no really. I had a harem of girls, all kinds: tall ones, short ones, sexy ones, and drop-dead gorgeous ones. I once traded twenty horses for a Greek Goddess. Man, just one look, and I was putty in her hands! In fact, she was the one that sent my camel to bed. She rode me all night long. Her tales of passion would curdle my toes and have the hair on my back stand at attention! I really can't go into detail. If the other fifty gals knew what we did, they would rebel, and leave me in the dust. All I would have left would be that stupid camel with the two humps. Not the kind of humps I want! hahaha ciao. The goddess is calling me, wooooooo hooooooo, so long!

I want to look my best when I win all those awards for all my accomplishments. What accomplishments? I see you don't read the tabloids or patronize book stores. It must be you got deep pockets and short arms. Well, enough about you. I'm going to have my star on that Hollywood Walk-A-Fame, win Pulitzers and that Porno Star of the Year statue. Yes, my acting debut in 'Jimmy Does Mrs. Chatterley' was my coming out. I can't wait till I do 'The Spanish Patient.' You talk about leaning her against the wall. Try leaning in the halls, on the floor, and up on the roof. Thank you and don't forget my newest book 'How I Became a Porno Star in You Tube' which will mesmerize you, to say the least, ciao!!

My fortune teller says I got the makings of a 'black magic man.' I don't know about no magic man and definitely not black. But I know I have many uncanny abilities. If you mess with me, I'll take a Polish pickle and stick it where it doesn't shine. Yep, up your butt! And if you try to cheat me, I'll feed you some zombie nuts for dinner. She was right, I'm not only crazy but lovable. Like Mel B, the 'America's got Talent' judge would say, "I'm off the Hook!"

Yes, I've done it all! I'm not too proud of everything I've done. But then you know if at first you don't succeed, try and try and try again. I've tried so many things! I don't know if I'm coming, going, or going in circles. Well, it's true because if Christopher Columbus hadn't tried we'd still be in the stone ages and King George the 23rd would still be sucking us dry for more tea taxes. Ray Charles would have never been discovered.

What have I contributed to society? Well, besides pockets on hats, mambo no. six, and my exotic recipes. I've got over a hundred patents. But it's not necessary to name them all. Even got an idea for a movie pilot about a masked woman who has a horse, and a side kick named Pronto who does everything fast. Damn, is he fast on the draw! Byeeeeeee Jimmy, aka Mr. Pronto.

Yes, I know about freedom. It's more than just another word. Picture yourself in a state of being where you can't roam around as you would like to. Have you ever been in prison? All you get is a few hours in the courtyard to feel the air and let it all hang out without bars, leg chains, or handcuffs. So don't tell me about freedom when you don't know what you got till you lose it. Especially if you are born in a dictatorship, where you are told what, where, when and why. Me, I would rather die than lose the most precious thing god gave us. Yes, it's called freedom! Never forget that for as long as you shall live . . .

I got to ask you a question. When do you know that you're a contender and it's time to kick it up a notch? Let me explain. When you're dating, you know, going out with girls in hopes of finding Ms. Right, and you think you've found a winner. Do you take the macho approach and grab her when you're escorting her home? And when you're about to part does the man come out of you, and you latch on to her like an octopus or do you gently take her hand, kiss it and off you go into the night? My buddies say I should be the aggressor, give her my all, and squeeze her good and tight! Whatever that means? But then I think, it's her who has to make the first move, pull you into her bosom and rub your face all over it. Oh well, tonight I'll try another approach. Perhaps, pat her booty whenever she passes by. If she tends to pass by a lot then that's the sign you've been hoping for. It's telling you that you're in like flint. Wish me luck! Tell you all about it some other day. Well, a man never tells, at least a gentleman that is! That's me—a gentleman through and through! And now a bona fide contender, ciao.

When I was a little bitty boy my sisters had to take me along if they wanted to go to the sock hops. You see my mother wanted me to chaperone those knuckleheads. Yeah, they were my deepest nightmares. They watched 'American Bandstand' every day after school. It was hosted by some dickhead named Dick Clark. As a result, I couldn't see Captain Kangaroo, Buster Crabbe, Jim Bowie, or Tarzan and all the cartoons, including Bozo, Mickey and Minnie, Daffy and Bugsy, and last but not least Popeye and Olive Oyl. So now they were going to pay if they wanted me to come along to the sock hops. Otherwise no deal! I requested a dime from each sister. I would buy me a pocketful of bubble gum. My pockets were filled to the brim. They danced every dance. Btw, I learned those steps too. I would hop on to the dance floor and all the girls would line up to take a shot at me. All the older boys hated me because their girls wanted me—a cute little hunk who could dance up a storm. I learned everything, from the lindy, the stroll, the hucklebuck, Willie & the hand jive, the twist, the mashed potato, Mickey's Monkey, the jerk, the barefooting, the limbo rock, the bossa-nova, the dog, the watusi, disco, and it didn't stop there. I could do all the modern dances too. Such as popping, breakdancing, the tango, el merengue, the mambo, the hokey pokey, the Macarena, and the list goes on and on. Nowadays, you can find me 'twerking' on YouTube videos. I tend to shake what my mama gave me! Who do you think gave the Evolution of Dance notoriety? Yep, me!!!

Folks, I got some great news. When you buy my book you are automatically entered in a drawing for a chance to win 'MY POOKIE IN A BOX.' That's her down below. What's so special about that little lady? Good question! She's the best bug repellant ever, and will rid you of rodents in the home. If not, I'll eat Pookie in a Macys store window. But that's not all! Here's the best part! When it's freaking cold outside, she'll keep your feet toasty hot. Oh, you haven't heard the end. You can kick her around the house. She'll always come back to you. So tell me what human does all those things for you. That's right, nada, zero, zilch! It proves the point—who needs a spouse when you got a Pookie Gyrl? What am I going to do without her? Have you ever heard of 'three dog night?' Yep, when it's cold outside I'll be sleeping with three dogs. What can I say? I'm brighter than a light bulb. Btw, you double your chances when you buy both books. Now that's what I call a good investment.

As you can see Pookie Gyrl loves boxes. No box is safe in my house!!!

Pookie once again in a box. That girl loves boxes, me, and you too! But you got to be in it to win her, and by all means buy five copies for your mother!!!

Somebody once asked me, "What is it that you want that you never had or did?" Well, besides getting my picture on the cover of the Rolling Stone, I wish I had a harem of girls like Hugh Hefner has in his mansion or those rich sheiks with all those camels and belly dancers. You see I want to be rich, famous, and have groupies knocking down my door wanting to party till I can't get enough. But I'm not going to hold my breath. You got to earn those perks and groupies. So when my books start to sell, then maybe I can hook up with the babes and party till I drop or can't find the door out, hahaha. Well, I'm going to put out an advertisement stating "Wealthy hunk—ok so I'm not wealthy but a hunk first class I am, thank you—looking for girls, seeking adventure, travel, and the good life. Send me your credentials, photos, front and back, c/o me to this station. Thank you. No, not Nick or Howie or Howard, they're for my eyes only!!!"

Folks, I've got something to tell you. I'm thinking of expanding my horizons, and running for some kind of political office. If you really must know, politicians are the most corrupt people on the face of the earth. They vote themselves to receive big, fat raises. They travel the world, eat at the finest restaurants, and all at the taxpayer's expenses. Best of all, they're always scratching each other's butts. That's why I would do well because I can be just as corrupt as the next guy! I'm an ass kisser by heart. Love to hold babies, and that sort of stuff. I'll get my friends and family members, all hooked up with high-paying jobs that require nothing or very little to do. Well, I was hoping you would all vote for me. They'll be something in it for you. A chicken in every pot, sexy girls, guys, and all the booze you can drink. My inauguration will be the most unforgettable party. I'll hire a bunch of strippers, male and female, so you can get your whistle wet or whatever else needs wetting. That definitely goes for you girls! Maybe we can party separately. I'll take you for a whirlwind, don't ask! So remember to vote for me! I'm leaving it all up to you, ciao, Jimmy, aka senator, mayor, governor, president. Who knows? Just call me god while you're at it because I'm Taylor made, and schooled by those Tammany Hall scoundrels. See ya, hate to be ya . . .

Do you remember that monkey story I told you about a few weeks back? My 'Kidnapper of Pets' for ransom business! Don't remind me. I'm thinking of getting a monkey. I plan to attach it to an organ push cart or whatchamacallit and charge folks for my visit. Like for a birthday party, a hen party, a school reunion, sweet 16, holiday celebration, a wedding, a divorce celebration, or whatever. Now the only problem is where am I going to get a monkey? It's got to be a newborn so I can train it to do my beck and call. The thought of me going over to Africa, or the everglades of Spain will no doubt cost me a bundle. I already spent a ton of money after that other monkey destroyed my house. I was thinking of going to a zoo and kidnap one. Yeah, I'll climb over the fence, but before I do that, I'll give the mama monkey bananas filled with sleeping pills. Oh, about fifteen pills in each banana to ensure that she doses off. Then I can snatch her baby. I know, what a great idea! I'll keep you in the loop as to my progress. I just know this is going to make me a fistful of dollars. Wish me luck!

That's the monkey I took from the Bronx Zoo. I bought him an outfit to blend in with the neighbors so they don't report me in to Animal Care and Control. His name is Jo Jo!

Can you keep a secret? As you are aware, I work part-time at that home improvement store. When I take my breaks, I mosey on down to the saw machine in aisle fourteen and make some extra bucks. How's that? I take a four inch by four inch by eight feet piece of wood, and chop it down into toothpicks. I know it's a tough job but somebody's got to do it. You can really say I'm a carpenter. I build toothpicks. When I go home my pockets are full of toothpicks. I sell them to restaurants so their customers can floss their teeth or the restaurants can use them to hold the triple deckers together. Hey, it helps pay the bills and fill my pockets with spending loot. Do me a favor, mums the word, see ya!!!

When I was 15 years old, in 7th grade, at JHS 126, my class was chosen to perform in the annual Shakespeare in the Auditorium event. I wanted so bad to take the lead as Romeo. I rehearsed my butt off for weeks. But the part of Romeo was given to George Hartofilis. I was devastated! I wanted to kick his ass! But George had a bunch of siblings, and in particular his sister Bertha. She was 17, and meaner than a junkyard dog! So I opted to be one of the stagehands instead. I schemed to make George a flop as Romeo.

For example, a ladder was placed where George would climb up to Juliet's balcony. He would eventually climb the shorter one and miss the window by two feet. I would lower the curtain at the wrong intervals and turn off the sound system at will. This caused havoc, and had everybody confused. The audience laughed it up a storm! Miss Leib would have expelled me from school if she knew I was the culprit for all the misfortunes. I can still recite Romeo's part, here check it out: "Juliet, Juliet where art thou! It is me Romeo, I'm the sun and you are the moon." Here's a bonus: "To be or not to be, that is the question!" And "Out spot, out!" And that's just from memory only! Maybe I should audition for the next Romeo and Juliet or Macbeth movie. I would win an Emmy or a Grammy no doubt about that! Ciao I got to rehearse some more. I'm a bit rusty but that won't be for long, byeeeeeeeee!!!!
(Play The Reflections "Just Like Romeo and Juliet")

Well, this has been one heck of a ride. I've lasted for a number of months. Passed the first audition in flying colors back in New Orleans. Then went on to Hollywood. I made the quarter finals, then the semifinals, and now I am down to the wire with the finals. Bet you're all wondering if I won. Well, you'll have to see the next episodes in 2014 to see where I stand. Bye bye, so long, farewell, and thank you all for allowing me to entertain you.

Thank you America and god bless each and every one of you!!!

Jimmy, aka Mr. Standup!!!

Other books written by author Jimmy Correa

NOTE: His first book, top left hand side, released in 2004 sold for $15.00 a pop can now fetch you any where from $70.00 to $576.00 depending on it's condition. That's like the price of gold hitting the roof. Maybe you should get all of them and buy five copies for your mother!!!!

Yours truly! You can visit me on my social media web site accounts listed below. We can chat, do business, lunch or twerk each other off!

1) You Tube—http://www.youtube.com/user/theloveman11378
2) Facebook—https://www.facebook.com/JimmysComedyShop?ref=hl
3) Pinterest—http://pinterest.com/jimmycorrea/boards/